Doorways to the Unseen 3

6 Tales of Terror and Suspense

James Dermond

Ambages Books

ISBN 978-1-946038-02-9

Cover art by Jeff Purnawan

*"From ghoulies and ghosties,
and long-leggedy beasties,
and things that go bump in the night,
Good Lord, deliver us!"*

- Scottish children's prayer

Contents

Creepy Jane   1

At Night's End   29

Cast in Amber   39

Cabin in the Woods   62

The Nest   74

Things that Go Bump in the Night   87

About the Author   101

Postscript   103

Creepy Jane

M iranda sat on the floor of the dimly lit bathroom, peering down into a silver hand mirror. She turned her head to view her profile, the palish light from a solitary candle casting foreboding shadows over her face. Miranda had never liked her own face very much; she wished instead that she resembled her mother or perhaps her sister, Samantha, blonde and glowing.

Miranda would turn eighteen next week and, the month after, graduate from high school. She frowned as black strands fell across her eyes and brushed them aside, her hair framing her oval face in a neatly cut veil. Miranda had been sitting on the bathroom floor almost since her classmate, Veronica, had left, gazing into the mirror she had found in her mother's dresser drawer.

"Really, just stare into the mirror," Veronica had told her, "and ask for 'Jane.' Wait a bit, and then say something like 'Jane, will I ever get married?' or 'Jane, will I ever fall in love?'" Veronica paused for a moment and raised an eyebrow, a faint smile playing on her lips. "Jane might even show you her frightening face after answering and ask, 'Do you think I'm pretty?' Don't hesitate. You'd better say 'yes' right away!"

Miranda leaned forward at the kitchen table and rested her arms across her textbook. "You're just trying to scare me," she said in an annoyed voice. "I don't believe a word of it."

Veronica held up both hands in protest and smiled again, this time breaking out into a broad grin. "My sister—you know, Melissa?—she swears it's all true. A friend of a friend told her the story. Says it happened at the friend of a friend's cousin's school all those years back. But why don't you just find out for yourself?"

Standing up from her seat at the table, Veronica looked around the kitchen. "I would use a hand mirror as you can just drop it if she shows you her ugly mug. Seeing Creepy Jane's face in the bathroom mirror would be way too scary."

Miranda had expected a quiet evening at home preparing for final exams but Veronica quickly began teasing her about boys. Dateless throughout high school, Miranda was set to begin college without ever having had a boyfriend. The two girls had known each other since middle school and their friendship was close, but there had always been a rivalry between them.

"School has just always been my priority." Miranda looked away defensively. "Besides, boys don't seem to like girls who are smarter than they are. And I'll remind you, you're the one struggling in pre-calc—even if you do have Tony."

Veronica said nothing, only smirking from the other end of the table.

"Whatever. Let's get this done," Miranda said brusquely. "Mom and Samantha are coming home from the recital in a couple of hours." Opening her pre-calculus textbook and reaching for her notes, she looked down at the papers with renewed focus.

"Have you ever heard of Creepy Jane?"

That was how it had all begun. Veronica had slumped in her chair, a physical expression of her disinterest in solving more math problems, her thin lips curved into a mischievous grin.

"Isn't that your aunt?" Miranda said without looking up from her textbook.

"No, silly, Creepy Jane is what they call an 'urban legend.' A story about some tragedy or some monster that no one can prove is real, but the story gets spread around anyway. But this one is real, believe me."

Miranda stopped leafing through her notes and glared at Veronica. "Do you want to pass this class or not?"

Veronica sat up in her chair and her smile vanished. "Okay, just let me tell you this one story and then we can get back to work. Is it a deal?"

Intrigued despite her better judgment, Miranda nodded silently. Veronica was a middling student, but she was quite creative and imaginative when the occasion presented itself.

Veronica looked away from the kitchen table, wrinkling her brow and pursing her lips. When she turned to face Miranda again, her eyes were piercing, holding a curious expression of genuine fear.

"Jane was a high school girl who lived many years ago—in the 1960s or something—and was mercilessly bullied by her classmates. She was awkward, with clunky glasses and braces on her teeth; homely to begin with but with looks made worse by having no style and no social skills.

"Jane had always been an outcast, but her abuse by the others reached a whole new level when she started high school. A group of mean girls a few grades ahead gave her the nickname 'Creepy Jane' and it stuck.

"One day, after being humiliated by these girls in front of the morning assembly, she went into the girls' restroom and ate rat poison—the entire box—which she had taken from the janitor's closet. A teacher found her dead in one of the stalls after she didn't show up for her afternoon class, her face horribly twisted and discolored.

"Soon after, those six girls who had bullied her the worst started to die or disappear one by one. Rumor had it that Creepy Jane's face would appear in their bathroom mirrors before each of them died or vanished, wearing that dreadful death mask the French teacher had found etched on her face. Within just months, all of the girls were either dead or gone. Never to be found."

Miranda swallowed despite herself, fighting off a tingling feeling creeping up her spine.

"The legend says that if a girl sits in a dark bathroom with a lit candle, stares into a mirror, and asks for Jane, she might just receive a reply from the spirit world," Veronica said. "Jane might be friendly, or she might not. That's the risk you take to know the future!"

Miranda stared at Veronica incredulously, the fingers of her right hand searching for a pencil.

Veronica was quiet for a moment, and then became insistent. "Really, just stare into the mirror and ask for Jane. Wait a bit, and then . . ."

Veronica waved as she opened her car door and then took a seat behind the wheel. Miranda stood on the porch steps, considering how much time she had left before Mom and Samantha walked in through the front door. Maybe an hour? More than enough time to find a mirror she could use to summon Creepy Jane. She scoffed to herself at the idea.

Miranda sat down on the living room couch and reached for the remote control, turning on the television. She started to watch a reality dating show, the light from the television set flickering in the otherwise dark room.

The young female contestant was asking each of the handsome, eligible bachelors a question about themselves. The last question the woman asked before the commercial break was "Have you ever been in love?"

Miranda fidgeted uncomfortably and turned to look over her shoulder at the entrance to the hallway, which ended at the first-floor bathroom's door. Shutting off the television, Miranda walked up the stairs to her mother's bedroom in the now-silent house. The spacious room was still cluttered with boxes from their recent move following her parents' divorce late last year.

Mom had taken some things she had found in their new home's attic and kept them here, somewhere in her room. Miranda remembered watching from the hallway outside as her mom put an ornate hand mirror into the dresser drawer.

Buried under layers of clothes in the bottom drawer, the mirror was wrapped in a white linen cloth. Miranda took the looking glass by its handle and held it in front of her. It was surprisingly weighty.

The mirror was made of sterling silver and appeared Victorian in origin. It was probably over a century old, with floral flourishes and a beveled edge. *Why would Mom have hidden the mirror here instead of just placing it on top of the dresser?* Miranda asked herself, perplexed.

Near the center of the mirror's back side was the image of a smiling young lady, her long, flowing hair framed by a wreath of flowers. Miranda decided such an antique object would be perfect for a séance with the spirit world—what better than the possession of some English lass now long dead?

Returning downstairs, Miranda took a candle in a small jar and a box of matches from the kitchen cupboard. She lit the candle on the bathroom sink countertop and then sat on a shaggy bathmat, squinting in the poor light at the mirror's round surface.

This is crazy! Miranda thought, nearly standing to put the mirror away in a drawer. Instead, her eyes searched the bathroom, glancing at the nylon shower curtain and the colorful bath towels hanging on the rack nearby. She took a deep breath and looked into the mirror once again.

"Jane?" Miranda said quietly, a nervous tremble in her voice.

Nothing.

"Jane?" Miranda said a second time, almost whispering. "Jane, will I meet my future husband at school?"

Silence.

The candle's flame flickered in its jar and the room grew darker for the briefest moment. Miranda's head turned quickly—she thought she'd heard a girl's laughter and then a soft sigh, but the sound had faded instantly.

A shape began to form within the mirror's frame. Miranda swallowed as she leaned forward, trying to make out its details. It was a person's face, but its features were too indistinct to tell who it might be. Slowly, the face of a girl came into hazy focus, smiling . . .

Sharon shook, her tears unending, her face buried in the wet palms of her hands. She heaved and gasped on the front steps of her home, her anguish palpable. A young police officer stood nearby, waiting for her to stop crying, if only for a moment.

"Here, Mrs. Ortiz, please take two of these with water," the officer said calmly, proffering two tablets in a packet and a foam cup. "Swallow them and then try to breathe normally, through your nose instead of your mouth. You may have a panic attack if you don't."

"I can't . . . I need to just sit here," Sharon managed, looking up at the officer through red, swollen eyes. "I can't go back inside the house!"

The officer nodded, her face a mask of understanding. "You won't need to, Mrs. Ortiz. A squad car will bring you and your daughter to the police station. A detective can take both of your statements there."

Sharon tore open the small paper package and tossed the tablets into her mouth before drinking. Several police cruisers were parked on the neighborhood street, their rolling lights flashing over the exterior of the house in the nighttime darkness. An ambulance had pulled up in the driveway and two paramedics were wheeling a covered gurney toward it.

Sharon's mind swam. She dropped the empty cup on the wooden step, which was the only thing she could really feel at this moment. In body and in soul, Sharon was numb everywhere; her eldest daughter, her beloved Miranda, was gone—strangled to death on the bathroom floor of their home.

The police officer helped Sharon to her feet and eased her aside as the paramedics passed them, the gurney rattling behind. They lifted it up the steps and disappeared into the house. Sharon heard a police body bag being zipped open and almost retched.

She turned her back on the scene and walked toward her daughter, Samantha. Samantha was speaking to a second police officer under the front lawn's tall, sheltering oak tree, who was hastily jotting notes down on a pad.

"Like I said, the front door and the bathroom door were both locked when we came home. Officer Williams and his partner had to force the bathroom door open with some tools after we called 911. That's when we found Miranda." Dried tears stained Samantha's face, but she had held her composure throughout the emergency call and even during the discovery of Miranda's body. Miranda's throat had been crushed as if with great force—Sharon imagined her daughter being strangled by some large and powerful escaped lunatic.

The officer put away his notepad and studied Samantha for a moment, wondering whether there might be more to this incident than the young girl was telling him. "There are no signs of forced entry either," he said, offering

Samantha another tissue from his shirt pocket. "Officer Williams searched both floors of the house, and the windows and doors are secure. You confirmed too that nothing appears to have been stolen."

The police officer briefly looked away to scan the house, and then met Samantha's gaze. "The only person who may have seen Miranda tonight other than you and your mother is Veronica Peters, her classmate at University High School. Is that right?"

Samantha saw her mother walking toward them. "That's right. Veronica and Miranda were supposed to study for finals tonight. Please call her parents and make sure Veronica made it back. I've got her number here somewhere..."

The paramedics wheeled Miranda's corpse out on the covered gurney and loaded it into the back of the waiting ambulance. Neither Sharon nor Samantha looked on as the paramedics did their work; both were still haunted by the nearly indescribable expression of horror on Miranda's face, her blood-saturated eyes staring up at the bathroom ceiling.

The police officer ushered Samantha and her mother back toward the house. Grim business indeed. He glanced again through the squad car's window at the clear evidence bag slung on the back seat. A strange antique mirror caught his eye, almost seeming to stare back at him.

"Yes, we've moved back in for now. No, I don't think we'll sell, especially if you say there's a chance a new lead might turn up. Thank you, Detective, I'll stop by the station some time for the mirror if you don't need to hold onto it any longer. It's a quite valuable heirloom—it belonged to the house's original owner. Thank you." Sharon hung up the phone and turned to Samantha.

"Your sister's case has been closed," she said quietly. "Detective Sherman says the department still has no solid leads. They're assuming it's a random killing at this point. The case is cold unless new evidence comes to light." She put a hand over her mouth and took a shaky breath as she searched Samantha's face for a reaction.

Samantha stood from her chair at the kitchen table and hugged her mother, the two embracing in silence for several long moments. Finally, Sharon gently pushed Samantha away and said in a reassuring voice, "We can keep hoping that something comes up. But we need to get on with our lives." Looking away with a pained expression, she added, "But your father won't be of any help to us. I haven't heard from him since the funeral."

Samantha sighed. "We don't need him. Dad's going to start a new family now that he's moved out of state. He'll forget about us, just you watch."

"Your father's wandering eye—and other body parts—are why we divorced to begin with," Sharon said, forcing a laugh.

Playing along, Samantha grinned. But the truth was that both she and her mother felt uneasy about moving back into the house. The police had spent days collecting forensic evidence, and a crime scene cleanup had been completed by a private company. It was, technically, all ready for them to move back in, but to Samantha it all felt too soon.

Neither she nor her mother was superstitious, but Miranda's death had been so violent... It was enough to threaten anyone's peace of mind. Detective Sherman had warned them that the killer was likely still out there and may even return. He'd ordered an increase in the number of neighborhood police patrols as a precaution.

The autopsy had found that only a hulking man with incredible physical strength could have caused Miranda's injuries. Yet, curiously, there were no marks or even fingerprints on Miranda's throat. The killer may have wrapped a towel around her neck before strangling her, but no towel with evidence of the crime was found and none were missing from the bathroom. And Miranda's face... Well, no one could forget such a frightful visage.

That Saturday, Samantha drove her mother's sedan to the local shopping mall to purchase some school supplies. Sharon's car now conspicuously displayed a sign stating "Student Driver," which was visible from both the front and rear of the vehicle.

Samantha parked near the movie theater and walked through a revolving glass door into the mall's lobby. Hurrying past the shops that lined the main thoroughfare, Samantha stepped onto the escalator. The office supply store was right at the top.

The woman behind the cash register smiled pleasantly at Samantha as she put notebooks and other supplies into a plastic bag. "Summer's almost over. Are you excited to be going back to school?"

"Sort of. I'll be glad to be out of the house," Samantha answered, looking past the woman to the shops on the opposite side of the mall's second floor. She spotted Miranda's old friend, Veronica, folding sweaters and shelving them on a display in the front window of a clothing store.

Samantha picked up her bag and hurried across the concourse, weaving through the shoppers passing her by. "I didn't know you worked here," Samantha said, stopping at the window display.

Veronica turned and seemed surprised. She put down the cotton sweater she was holding and managed a half-smile. "Samantha, hi. How are things coming along? I haven't seen you since Miranda's funeral back in April."

Samantha was immediately taken aback by how fatigued Veronica appeared; there were bluish-dark circles under her eyes and fine creases around her mouth. "Mom and I moved back into the house this week," she replied. "I'm getting ready for the school year. We're trying to get back to normal, but it's hard."

"You're not afraid to live there after what happened?" Veronica said, with legitimate concern. She then looked over her shoulder as if searching for a manager—or perhaps, Samantha thought suddenly, someone else—who might be watching them.

"We don't have much of a choice, really. Mom just bought the house, and we'd have to sell at a huge loss. Miranda's death was on the news for like a whole week." Samantha gave a deflated sigh. "Every real estate agent would tell their buyers about what happened. The house is a no sell."

Veronica nodded weakly. Samantha couldn't get over it— the girl had utterly changed since Miranda's burial service several months ago. Veronica seemed not only tired, but truly exhausted, almost entirely drained of her usual good humor and vitality. She seemed now a liminal figure, as if steadily fading away, from the daylight and into the shadows.

"I don't want to sound crazy, but don't you believe in ghosts?" Veronica's smile persisted, but Samantha could tell she was quite serious.

Samantha stiffened. "No, I don't. And neither does Mom. Living in a murder house is a bit spooky, but dead is dead."

Veronica's eyes suddenly darted left and right as Samantha uttered this last phrase.

"Mom keeps the first-floor bathroom shut tight, but only because we don't want to use it," Samantha continued. "It's too painful for us right now. Maybe someday we'll open it back up, but not any time soon."

"I believe in ghosts," Veronica said softly. "I do."

"Veronica, is something wrong? I mean, are you sick or something?"

"No, why would you say that?" Veronica forced a wider smile and hopped slightly—a feeble attempt to perk herself up.

"You just seem different from when I saw you last. Like you're not getting enough rest."

"Oh, I'm just a bit worried about starting college next month," Veronica said, waving a hand dismissively. "Excited and worried. Sleep has taken a back seat to getting ready for my first semester away from home." Veronica looked away again, as if afraid to say more.

"I have to get going," Samantha said slowly, backing away. "School is starting for me too. My junior year at Uni High." Samantha snickered nervously. "I bet you won't miss that place."

Veronica changed the subject instead of answering. "Do the police have any new leads or is it pretty much done?" She seemed hopeful now, more engaged than she had been for much of their conversation.

"It looks like it's done," Samantha answered. "Whoever did it needs to be caught, but the police have nothing to go on. They even took that funny mirror Mom kept in her room as evidence, but found no fingerprints other than Miranda's."

"You said a mirror? What kind of mirror?" Veronica instantly became animated, her deadened eyes widening.

"An old hand mirror. It's... some antique that came with the house," Samantha said as she furtively glanced at her wristwatch. "Our agent told us only one other family lived in the house between us and the original builders: a married couple with four boys. The family left everything in the attic alone, even though they knew some of the things stored there were probably collector's items."

Veronica fell into silence. A few customers passed by them as the girls conversed, but none interrupted.

"When we were studying that night, before I left, I told Miranda about Creepy Jane." Veronica now seemed on the verge of tears.

Samantha frowned. "Who or what is Creepy Jane?"

"I told Miranda it was an urban legend, but it was just a story I made up on the spot," Veronica said, sniffling as she wiped a closed eye with her fingers. "I wanted to scare her a bit, just for fun. But she may have tried what I told her to do."

"You told her to look into a mirror?"

"Not just that, but to call for Jane while gazing into a mirror in a dark bathroom. Don't use the bathroom mirror, I said—light a candle, and then call for Creepy Jane. Ask Jane if she'll find you a husband while staring into the mirror." Veronica managed a small smile as she recited the instructions. "It's nonsense, of course, but something might have gone wrong. I never told the police when they questioned me because I didn't think it was important."

"I doubt that mirror has anything to do with it," Samantha countered. "The bathroom door was locked from the inside—that's the part the police detective couldn't figure out. They don't know how the killer got in there in the first place."

Veronica shivered and pulled at her button-down sweater. "I'd move out if I were you," she said in a hollow voice. "You shouldn't stay in that house. It's not safe for you and your mom."

Samantha was unshaken by this revelation about her sister's death. "The mirror is just an old mirror, Veronica," she offered. "Miranda probably wanted to store it away in the bathroom drawer when she was attacked... or whatever happened."

Veronica hugged Samantha tightly and said, "I'll see you at Christmas when I get back from school. Take care of yourself. And don't worry about me. I'll be fine."

Bemused, Samantha walked toward the escalator and briefly wondered if she should examine that odd silver mirror once Mom retrieved it from the police station.

"Why would Veronica fill your head with a crazy story like that? I'm not surprised, though. I always thought that girl was a liar." Becca sat with Samantha and their friends at the picnic table, interjecting right after Samantha finished her tale. "Creepy Jane sounds about as real as Veronica's bustline," Becca declared, her manner as mocking as ever.

Lily and Ava snorted with laughter as Samantha shifted uncomfortably. Becca had called late in the afternoon and suggested she and the girls "hang out" at the park near Samantha's house that evening. School would start again in a few weeks, and everyone wanted to savor the last vestiges of warm summer weather before they had to once again spend all day sitting in a classroom.

"It's just... it's so strange. Why would Miranda have had Mom's hand mirror with her unless she really was trying to contact Creepy Jane? There's a lighted vanity mirror above the sink. If she were combing her hair or something, she would have used the bathroom mirror." Samantha looked around at her friends, genuinely worried that the circumstances of Miranda's death could be even more bizarre than anyone had previously imagined.

The small public park was mostly empty; only a few couples and cyclists passed by in the distance. Becca smiled and reached across the picnic table to touch Samantha's hand reassuringly. "Veronica may somehow be blaming herself for your sister's death. You said she looked wiped out, like she's not getting enough sleep. Maybe she's 'remembering' things that never really happened."

Samantha examined the youthful faces of the girls, all of whom she had known since childhood. *What do they think of me now?* Samantha considered. There had been an outpouring of sympathy from her classmates and neighbors following Miranda's murder, but there was, she knew, a limit to any grieving period. Samantha had been hesitant to share what she had been told by Veronica, but she'd needed to tell someone of her fears, her growing suspicion that something very peculiar had occurred that night.

"I have an idea. Let's break into the school and see if Creepy Jane shows up in the restroom mirror when we call for her. Then we'll know if Veronica is telling the truth or if it really is just an urban legend." Jumping up from her seat on the bench, Becca smiled at the other girls in the receding twilight. "It'll be some wicked fun before we're sent off into slavery again." She clapped her hands together with glee as she spoke.

"You're an idiot. We'll be caught and suspended before school even starts. Sit back down or go home." Ava shook her head, exasperated. "This 'Creepy Jane' is an urban legend; there's nothing to it," she said scornfully.

"I've climbed through one of the pool building windows before with Aaron Rogers," Becca said slyly. "We went swimming at night and then escaped through the side door near the offices. That old janitor, Carl, is too careless to lock everything up, especially the windows."

Becca began to walk toward her waiting SUV and waved at her friends to follow her. "I'm going, even if none of you are," she said over her shoulder, passing the sand-covered playground near the picnic tables. "If there's nothing to it then at least we'll get to go for a swim in the pool."

Lily stood up and followed Becca without saying anything. She had been observing their banter but had only become engaged when Becca announced her plans for a midnight swim. Ava looked over at Samantha, who glanced at her, smiled apologetically, and then stood up to follow Becca. Rolling her eyes, Ava followed.

"Hold my flashlight, will you?" Becca said, thrusting it to Lily as she crouched near the window. "I'll climb through." Becca dropped her compact gym bag onto the grass in front of her before pulling the frame of the large, partially open awning window outward, its ill-maintained hinges creaking.

The crank window's stiff hinges held in place, allowing Becca to squeeze under the frame and carefully drop down onto the pool room's blue-tiled floor. Standing at the edge of the full-length swimming pool, Becca looked around and then motioned for Lily to throw her gym bag through.

Becca bent over to pick up her bag and then walked behind the diving board, pushing open the door to the girls' locker room. The reflection of the dimmed ceiling lights on the water sent a kaleidoscope of rippling shapes spinning across the tiled walls of the pool room.

Lily turned to Ava and Samantha who were standing watch behind her and whispered, "Come on, Becca said to wait by the coach's office." The three girls walked around the length of the school natatorium and found the path to the building's side door. They then waited patiently in the dark for Becca to appear.

Soon, the metal door clicked and then slowly opened. Becca was standing in front of them in a one-piece swimsuit, beaming from ear to ear. "Get inside, someone might see you!" she breathed hurriedly. "I'm going to do some laps around the pool before we try our phone call to the dead."

Samantha closed the door behind them and followed the girls down an unlit hallway past several locked offices and into the pool room. Becca lowered herself into the chlorinated water, attempting not to make too much noise. She did a few laps and then swam in broad circles, drifting through the water on her back as she paddled with her arms.

Lily sat on one of the wooden benches placed against the walls and took off her sneakers and socks. She stripped down to her underwear and then stepped into the pool, dropping down into the water with an audible *plop* and vanishing beneath its surface. She bobbed up a moment later and grinned, pushing back her long, wet hair with her hands.

Ava and Samantha took seats on a wooden bench at the opposite side of the pool, watching Becca and Lily eagerly muck about. After a short while, Samantha glanced at Ava and the two of them stood and walked toward the girls' locker room.

Samantha purposely left the lights off as they entered to not risk attracting the attention of Carl the janitor. Becca had set down her gym bag on one of the benches dividing two rows of metal lockers; Samantha easily found the neon-colored bag even in the semi-dark. The locker room was deathly quiet, with only the distant sound of splashing breaking the silence.

"Becca said she put the candle and matches from the SUV's compartment in here," Samantha noted as she unzipped the bag's top and began to fish around inside. "Her dad insists she keep an 'emergency' candle with a box of matches in the SUV in case of a blizzard."

Ava laughed. "There hasn't been snow in the Central Valley in probably ten years."

"You're right. But she goes skiing with her family up in the mountains. You never know when a candle might come in handy."

Samantha unscrewed the circular lid and saw that three wicks were embedded in the candle's wax surface. She placed the open tin on the grooved rail running beneath the bench's wall-mounted mirror. Ava looked over her shoulder, catching Samantha's eyes in the mirror. "Sam," she said hastily. "The splashing's stopped."

Samantha listened. "They must be out of the pool. Go grab them so we can do this. The longer we stay, the more we're pushing our luck."

"But this is a real thrill, right?" Ava replied, her smirking face only faintly visible. "See you in a moment."

As Ava left, the locker room door creaked open and then closed with a thud. Samantha looked around in the dark, not truly afraid but beginning to feel a chill. The door to the locker room opened again.

"Ava?" she called.

No response, no footsteps—nothing but the sound of the door swinging shut.

There was a dark shape standing at the end of the lockers, watching her. Samantha squinted. "Yes, Ava, very funny. Come on, where are the others?"

The figure moved across the open space between the rows of lockers, disappearing behind them. Samantha swallowed. She rubbed her hands over her forearms and slowly stepped forward to peer around the edge.

Nothing was there. The chill in the air had become more pronounced.

Then, movement out of the corner of her eye. Samantha spun and caught a glimpse of the back of a girl's head, long tresses flowing as she disappeared through the now-open locker room door.

As the door swung closed, it was almost immediately pushed open from the outside. Ava, Lily, and Becca stepped into view, giggling amongst themselves. Samantha faced them and saw that Lily and Becca had wrapped towels around their midsections. Lily was grasping her clothes and the collars of her sneakers with both hands.

"Hey, let's get this done. Light that candle," Becca said, coming to a stop in front of the face-level rectangular mirror. "We'll be dried off soon."

Samantha blinked and put a hand over her throat as she turned to light the candle. Beginning to wonder if she should mention the uncanny figure she'd seen, she paused. Certainly, if someone had really walked through that door, her friends would have noticed. *Veronica's paranoia is finally getting to me*, she thought, pushing the notion away.

The four girls lined up in front of the locker room mirror, reflections of their shadowy faces smiling in the soft candlelight. "This is like one of those 'dead teenager' movies," Becca gasped sardonically. "Let's hope nothing's in here stalking us!"

"Don't say that," Samantha scolded in a coarse whisper. "We'll all ask for Jane at once and then repeat it at least ten times. I'll start and then all of you join in right away."

The others nodded.

"Jane?" Samantha said in a low voice as she gazed into the long mirror. The others chimed in almost simultaneously. "Jane?" they said, Becca and Lily smiling broadly as they intoned the ghost's name.

"Jane? Are you there, Jane? Please answer us," Samantha said.

By their twelfth attempt, her voice had grown pleading.

"Nothing going to happen. Let's go before we get caught," Becca said with some relief. She reached down for her gym bag and pulled out her jeans and t-shirt.

Just then, a gust of air passed over the flames of the melting candle, its fires dancing briefly. For a moment, Samantha could see the outline of a small, blurred shape coming into focus within the depths of the mirror.

A door slammed open outside in the pool room. The sound of a mop bucket on wheels being pushed over the tiled floor cut through the silence.

"It's Carl! Put out the light!" Becca said as she snuffed the candle's flames between her fingertips. Lily grabbed her clothes from the bench and wadded them into Becca's bag.

This done, the two of them quickly slipped on their sneakers.

Becca dropped the spent candle into a plastic trash barrel. "There's an open window in here somewhere. I definitely felt a breeze when we first walked in."

Hurrying to the back of the dark locker room, Becca spied an open awning window above the sinks and toilet stalls. She waved the other girls over.

"Stand on me and then pull me up last," Becca whispered, half-enjoying the prospect of being caught. Ava nodded, clambered up Becca's braced body, and placed her feet on the taller girl's athletic shoulders. Panting, Ava slipped through the window, followed by Lily with Becca's gym bag, and then, lastly, Samantha.

The wheels of the mop cart had grown loud, and the door to the locker room abruptly flung open, bright light shining onto the rows of locker units. Lily and Samantha grabbed Becca's arms as she flailed desperately on the tips of her sneakers, and then pulled her roughly through the crevice under the window's pane.

They ran over the nighttime grounds of the school natatorium toward the parking lot. Breathing hard, the girls piled through the car's unlocked doors, Becca quickly starting the engine. In an instant, they were pulling out toward the lot's exit and the street beyond.

"That was close!" Becca shouted as they rode off, all smiles at their getaway. "But—admit it—it was loads of fun too! Just don't tell anyone—at least, not this semester."

Samantha looked out the backseat window of the sleek SUV as her friends talked and laughed, the late-night summer breeze blowing about her as they drove past tracts of suburban homes. *Did I really see something in the mirror?* Samantha worried, an uneasiness gripping her. *Or was it all just nerves?*

Placing a small stack of books on the library table in front of her, Samantha seated herself and took a deep breath, mentally preparing to dive into the volume at the top of the pile: *Urban Myths and Legends*, a hardcover book by some author she had never heard of. The books were mostly older, some several decades old, but these worn texts were all she'd been able to find in the local library's catalog database.

A quick Internet search earlier had revealed almost nothing about Creepy Jane except a few creepypastas, none of which identified Creepy Jane by name. The books Samantha had pulled from the library shelves turned out to contain much more detail, but still made no mention of an urban legend centered around a dead girl called "Creepy Jane."

Over hours, Samantha read stories about some creature named the Slenderman; ghostly hitchhikers; black-eyed children (this one really scared her); an ax murderer dubbed "The Bunny Man"; and various tales of gateways to Hell hidden in abandoned buildings, hotel rooms, and other out-of-the-way places. But no Creepy Jane.

Had Veronica been telling the truth about making the story up, or had she lied to cover something up? Samantha sighed. She could never tell with Veronica. Like Becca said, that girl was a liar, and you never did know with her.

But something stood out in Samantha's memory of that night that continued to push her to question the events surrounding Miranda's death. As the police report recorded, there'd been no sign of forced entry and no unidentified fingerprints anywhere. The bathroom door had been locked from the inside. Each of these occurrences was hard to explain but, taken together, they were very strange indeed. There was something else too, half-buried in the back of Samantha's mind...

Officer Williams pressed his ear against the bathroom door a second time, hoping against hope that Miranda might answer him. After a moment, he reached into a heavy bag at his feet and removed a metal implement and a sledgehammer. His colleague, Officer Sanchez, stepped up and wedged the two-pronged fork at the implement's head between the door and its frame, then stepped aside as Officer Williams struck with the hammer. The sharp points of the head drove deep into the door's narrow gap, forming a wedge.

Both officers leveraged their weight against the entry tool's handle, prying the bathroom door open with a crack. Samantha rushed past the two men and stood over her sister; Miranda was sprawled on her back on the tile floor. Light from the hallway spilled over the dead body and glinted off a silver mirror lying face up next to the corpse. Samantha glanced down into the mirror's surface and saw someone staring back at her...

"Samantha, step away! Outside, now!" Officer Williams reached over and grabbed Samantha's arm, leading her out of the bathroom. "Stay with your mother," he said. When he returned, Officer Sanchez was checking Miranda for vital signs.

The events of that night jumbled together in Samantha's mind. At first, she'd dismissed what she had seen as a trick of the light, had convinced herself that the face was her own somehow distorted. But that face, it hadn't been a normal face—it was the face of someone evil...

Samantha's phone vibrated on the wood laminate table, pulling her attention back to the present moment. Mom was calling her, probably about the car. It was already early afternoon and Mom had wanted to do some shopping before the weekend. *I'll just let it go to voicemail*, Samantha thought absent-mindedly.

What if it's our house? A chill crept over Samantha. Pulling up a browser on her phone, she hurriedly searched records of their town's past for anything tragic. When nothing came up, she searched for her address. And before long, she found something.

More than half a century ago, another murder took place near the grounds of their new home, also involving a young girl. The girl had been strangled to death. The website mentioned the area surrounding their house had once been an apple orchard, with the house the only residence for several miles.

Olivia Radcliff was the murdered girl's name. She'd been the fourteen-year-old daughter of Helen Radcliff, a well-to-do widow. Mrs. Radcliff regularly hired an immigrant named Giuseppe Rosini as a gardener and to pick apples in the orchard. Giuseppe spoke little English, and he was grateful for the work.

Mrs. Radcliff arrived home one summer afternoon to find Olivia missing. She searched the orchard and discovered Olivia among the rows of flowering apple trees, bleeding from her temple. There had been a struggle, and someone had strangled her until she died.

The police were quick to blame Mr. Rosini, who had neither an alibi nor the funds for a proper legal defense. An investigation into Mr. Rosini's past found he had attempted assault on a teenage girl in his home country before fleeing to avoid prosecution. The trial jury convicted him on only circumstantial evidence and Mr. Rosini was executed by hanging soon after.

Samantha slowly scrolled through the website's article and examined the embedded black and white photographs of Mrs. Radcliff and Olivia. Olivia was very beautiful—she wore a wide-brimmed straw hat and summer dress, her outstretched hand resting on the branch of an apple tree, but there was something quite disturbing about the picture itself.

The longer Samantha looked at the girl in the photo, the more she was taken by an unnatural coldness in the girl's aspect. Outwardly she was lovely, but there was something terribly cruel about the way she gazed back at the camera, or at whoever had taken that picture. Stranger still was Olivia's resemblance to herself; the girl could have been

Samantha's long-lost sister from another era, the two were so similar in appearance.

"I'm so glad you called ahead. Visitor hours are almost done for today. But how did you find Mrs. Radcliff's address?" The young nurse led Samantha down a long hallway at the convalescent home, turning to smile at her intermittently.

"It wasn't hard," Samantha said. "Almost everyone's address is somewhere on the Internet if you know where to look." She glanced at her wristwatch: it was late afternoon. She had left her phone in the car as she was certain Mom would call her again.

"Mrs. Radcliff is our community's only centenarian; she's been here for I don't know how many years. You're the first guest she's had since I started here." The nurse stopped in the open doorway to the visitors' lounge and briefly gestured toward a very aged woman slouched in a wheelchair. The old woman looked down at the floor, seeming not to notice Samantha and the nurse's presence.

The nurse continued to speak in a quiet, almost sympathetic voice as the two watched Mrs. Radcliff from the doorway. "She's nearly blind now, just so you know, but she still has her faculties. You can visit with her here in the lounge. It'll be empty except for the two of you."

The nurse approached Mrs. Radcliff's wheelchair and leaned over to speak into her ear. "Mrs. Radcliff, this is your visitor, Samantha. She says she lives in your old house now with her mother."

Mrs. Radcliff looked up in Samantha's direction, her sightless eyes dull and opaque. "Yes? Samantha, please sit down in front of me so I can better hear you." Her voice still held some strength, even though her body was clearly failing.

"I hope you find out what you need for your summer project. I'll be back in thirty minutes." The nurse walked away casually, partially closing the door to the lounge behind her as she left.

The old woman wobbled her head as if trying to get her bearings before she spoke. "You live in my house on Rosewood Lane? Is that what you want to talk about?" Mrs. Radcliff seemed calm, but there was a hint of apprehension in her tone.

"Yes, there's a silver hand mirror my mother found in the attic. I think it may have belonged to your daughter, Olivia." Samantha studied Mrs. Radcliff's blotted and wrinkled face, thinking back to the photograph of her as a young woman.

Mrs. Radcliff continued to move her head back and forth but said nothing. After a long moment, she said, "Olivia? What do you know of my daughter?" Visibly agitated, a pallor of fear began to spread over the old woman's already ashen complexion.

"There's an image of a smiling girl wearing flowers in her hair on its back," Samantha explained. "Did you give that mirror to Olivia?"

"No," Mrs. Radcliff replied forcefully. "The mirror was mine when I was a girl, a gift from my own mother. Olivia would take it from my room and admire herself for hours. What a vain child she was."

Samantha waited a moment and then said, "I think Olivia may be trying to contact us from the afterlife." She leaned forward in the lounge chair after she spoke, waiting to hear Mrs. Radcliff's reaction to her claim about the supernatural.

Mrs. Radcliff again sat in silence, her head wobbling about. When she replied to Samantha, her raised voice was scalding, her words sharp and acerbic. "Olivia was born wicked. I could see the cruelty in her from early on, but her wickedness grew worse as she began to reach womanhood." Mrs. Radcliff's brow furrowed, as if she were in great pain.

"Animals would go missing from the neighbors' farms. Then, one day, a young boy vanished. Olivia said he had run away, but his body was later dredged up from the woods nearby. His body was...

"I found Olivia alone in the orchard. Her back was to me, standing among the trees not yet ready for the fall harvest. As she turned, she held something clenched in her hand.

"I stuck Olivia across the head with the butt of an ax. An ax I'd found in our shed, wrapped in rags, dried blood on its blade and on its handle.

"Olivia fell, and I knelt down to choke my daughter for what she had done. She fought. Oh, how she fought! Then, finally, her evil life was choked out of her."

Samantha sat motionless in the chair, stunned by this almost involuntary confession. Mrs. Radcliff gazed directly at Samantha, her thin brows arched, her milk-white eyes narrowing as if attempting to focus.

With a fierceness belying her frail appearance, Mrs. Radcliff suddenly reached forth with a bony hand and gripped Samantha's wrist, holding her fast. "But evil never truly dies," the old woman breathed. "Evil will always find a way to continue on, if it can."

The old woman closed her eyes under heavy lids and sank back into her wheelchair, exhausted. She released her grasp on Samantha's arm.

Samantha stood, eyes wide, and hurried away to find the nurse.

Samantha leaned against the open car door, rubbing her tender wrist. Her phone now showed two voicemail messages from Mom.

I'll listen to them while I'm driving back, Samantha thought contritely. *Mom must be pissed by now.*

As she pulled out of the parking lot, the first voicemail played from the phone's speakers. *"Hello, Sam, this is Mom. You're still not back from the library, so I'm going to step out with Veronica Peters' mother, Carol. She called me and said Veronica has serious insomnia, can't sleep. Carol thinks it has to do with Miranda, but Veronica won't say. Talk to you soon."*

Samantha deleted the first voicemail with her free hand as she drove and then let the second message play. *"Hello, Sam. This is Mom again. I hope you're OK. I'm back from coffee with Carol. She's really upset. She's afraid Veronica won't start college in a few weeks and doesn't know what to do. Carol also dropped by the police station with me on the way home and I picked up my mirror from evidence. Talk to you soon."*

Samantha took a deep breath and began to drive faster along the expressway. By the time she pulled into her driveway, the waning summer sun was setting below the horizon, casting long shadows from the nearby trees over their home.

The front door was unlocked. Samantha stepped into the silent house and closed the door behind her.

"Mom? Are you there?" Samantha called out. "I'm sorry I didn't call you back. I took another trip after the library."

She put her phone down on the kitchen table and looked around. "I really need to see that mirror you brought back with you," she called out again. "It's important."

Samantha turned the corner into the dim hallway, the last light of the day falling through the living room windows onto the rug. The bathroom door at the end of the hall was cracked open, a flickering light coming from inside the otherwise dark space.

Samantha stopped. "Mom?"

The bathroom door swung open and Sharon hurtled from the darkness, grabbing Samantha by the throat. Mother and daughter tumbled onto the hardwood floor,

Sharon's icy cold hands violently clutching Samantha in a vise-like grip. Her eyes bulging with madness, Sharon tightened her stranglehold, a manic, gape-mouthed grin on her face.

Pinned on her back, Samantha's mouth fell open as she struggled to swallow one more breath. The image of her mother above her, hands around her throat, grew blurry as darkness closed in...

"Hello, there's a medical emergency at 1211 Rosewood Lane. My mother's had a heart attack. No, she's not responding to me. I'm sorry, I can't tell. Please send an ambulance."

Samantha put her phone down on the kitchen table. She stepped over Sharon's body in the hallway and walked into the bathroom, flipping on the light switch. The silver mirror lay on the bathroom rug, its glass surface unmarred and intact.

Samantha touched the mirror fondly and then admired her own reflection, tucking a loose lock of blonde hair behind an ear. Then, wrapping the antique piece in its white linen cloth, she placed it at the bottom of the dresser drawer for safekeeping.

At Night's End

Ferdinando's wife labored nearby as he lay on the floor of their one-room apartment. He watched her; she had not noticed him awaken. Isabella's back was to Ferdinando, her attention engaged by some chore. Without turning, Isabella hastily picked up a bundle and then left, shutting the rickety door to their tenement room behind her.

Did we fight again? I can't remember, Ferdinando thought to himself as he pushed aside the worn blankets he lay beneath and looked out the window. Isabella was now hurrying down the cobbled street in front of the tenement, visible only because of the hanging lantern lights stationed along the street's passage.

Ferdinando breathed deeply at the open window from the night air of the city. The fourth-floor apartment offered a sprawling view of the tops of the squalid dwellings and domed structures around the city's center, among which nighttime denizens made their way through narrow streets. Isabella's figure had grown more distant, but Ferdinando was still able to see her disappear through the door of a church not far from their tenement.

A wave of nausea washed over Ferdinando, forcing him to steady himself against the windowsill. Ferdinando believed he was recovering from a long sickness, a fever that had held him down and ravaged his body as well as his mind. Even though the delirium had subsided, Ferdinando sometimes felt as if he were suffocating. Occasionally, he even felt confused as to his whereabouts.

Ferdinando grabbed at the loose linen shirt he was wearing. This was not his usual sleeping attire. He looked around. None of his clothes or other belongings were visible. *How long have I been asleep?* Ferdinando worried, noting the now threadbare walls around him.

Ferdinando reached under the bottom of a wooden cabinet, one of the last pieces of furniture left in the room. He produced a pair of flat leather shoes, a gift from his brother in Florence.

Isabella didn't know about these, Ferdinando thought, congratulating himself on his foresight. *But even with new shoes, I'm dressed like a peasant.* Ferdinando sat on the floor and slipped on the simple footwear before heading out onto the street.

Two armed guards from the city night watch, glowing lanterns in hand, passed Ferdinando as he made his way through the city streets. The church Isabella had entered earlier was dedicated to Saint Vitalis of Milan, an early martyr to the faith, whose feast day had passed a few months ago. Climbing to the top of the stone steps, Ferdinando pulled at the heavy door handle of the church's entranceway and walked inside.

Isabella was kneeling near the front of the church, only a few pews from the altar. The place was mostly deserted at this time of night, but the last remaining faithful, communicants who had not yet left for bed, continued to keep a vigilant schedule.

Ferdinando seated himself in the back near a wrought-iron stand and watched the flames of its rows of tallow candles slowly dwindle. The church was dark, but its subdued, shadowy interior was somehow comforting. Ferdinando thought about Isabella and what might have impelled her to come here so late. *Is she praying for me to recover from my illness?*

Feeling dizzy, Ferdinando leaned back in the pew and his mind wandered, his attention slipping away. He recalled when he and Isabella had eloped and then married in secret, her wealthy Florentine merchant father livid at the idea of their union in holy matrimony. As he drifted off into a reverie all his own, Ferdinando thought he heard Isabella crying softly in the distance...

"No, I forbid it. He'll make a pauper out of you and a fool out of me," Isabella's father commanded, ignoring his daughter's tears.

"I'll never marry Signor Altoviti! I swear it!" Isabella cried out, sobbing, her face half-buried in the cushions of a chair. She looked up defiantly from the carpet-strewn floor of her father's study.

"Your beloved holds large debts, Isabella. He owes creditors, dangerous men." Signor Ruspoli turned away and looked out over the inner courtyard of the family's villa, considering all that his daughter would sacrifice for romantic love should she fail to obey him.

The sound of the church door closing shook Ferdinando into wakefulness. Peering ahead, he saw that Isabella was gone from her spot at the pew.

Ferdinando opened the church door and looked out into the vacant street. Isabella was already well ahead of him, headed away from the church, her bundle from their apartment under an arm.

Following from the shadows, Ferdinando watched her stop at a nighttime shop, a garment-makers. The old man behind the shop counter opened Isabella's bundle, examining what appeared to be articles of clothing under the light of a hanging lamp.

Ferdinando heard a child's voice speak from behind him: *"Signore,* are you looking for something?"

He turned and saw a young boy, a street urchin, standing a few paces away. The boy was ill-kept and wore a puzzled expression on his anemic face. "You seem lost, *signore*," the boy reiterated, stepping toward Ferdinando.

Before answering, Ferdinando looked back over his shoulder for Isabella. The shopkeeper was stowing something away, his back to the store counter. Isabella was no longer there.

"Come with me, *signore*. There is a show tonight. A special show for those who walk at midnight." The ragged boy began to scamper away, gesturing with a grimy hand for Ferdinando to follow.

Pausing, Ferdinando thought of returning to the apartment to see if Isabella was there. *If she is, she'll be in no mood to see me*, he surmised. *I'll wait until she falls asleep before heading back to home*. Ferdinando followed the urchin into the dingy alleyways of the city, fearful but also excited at what he might find.

The two night travelers stalked past tenement slums, closed shops, and shuttered trattorias until, at last, Ferdinando was forced to stop, gasping for air. He swallowed a jagged breath, the moist atmosphere of the summertime city causing his weakened lungs to labor and groan.

The urchin descended a long flight of stairs near a wine shop, slipping around a sharp corner as he reached the bottom. Ferdinando staggered after him, trying to keep pace with his now-silent guide.

As he turned into an alleyway, Ferdinando saw the boy standing at its far end, a small figure in the unlit corridor. The urchin waved his hand yet again, beckoning Ferdinando.

At the end of the covered alleyway was an aperture that gave way to a dilapidated amphitheater, itself open to the night sky and half-ringed by roughly hewn wooden benches. The nexus of the amphitheater was a raised stage, its rear obscured by house curtains.

"Here, *signore*. You will sit here." The urchin pointed to an elevated bench not far from the forestage that offered a good view of the center stage. Ferdinando took his seat and looked around as the urchin climbed the steps and disappeared behind the stage's blanched and tattered red curtains. There was no one else to be seen.

There were no lights in the amphitheater—only the gauzy rays of the overhead moon lit the stage. Ferdinando made a long, wheezing cough into his open palm. He then sucked in a trembling breath, hoping to himself that his sickness wouldn't interrupt the performers.

Without warning, the stage curtains parted, revealing six masked men dressed in costume. They lit pitch torches and then whirled them, streaking the darkness with fiery trails of sparking embers. The men concluded their brief spectacle by placing the torches in ornate upright stands situated along the front of the stage, illuminating its center.

Once the torches were set, acrobats and actors emerged from the wings adorned in jeweled masks and full theatrical costumes. The performers unfurled a large white sheet, which was then held at the corners by the troupe members. A stately actor, resplendent in the faded grandeur of his attire, stepped onto the forestage and addressed the audience of one: "Welcome to *Il Teatro delle Ombre, signore*." His voice shattered the night's silence. "Here, at the Theater of Shadows, we will tell you a story. One with caricatures of the real world, as shown behind the Veil of Memory. Watch closely, *signore*— your fate may depend on it."

The man stepped back after finishing his oration, disappearing into the folds of the nearly translucent white sheet, leaving no shadow. Two puppeteers holding marionettes on strings followed, ducking behind the raised sheet. The silhouettes of animated figures appeared, both finely dressed men.

The voice of the regal actor was now heard again, this time seeming to project from nowhere. "A young man and his elder brother were good friends, close from an early age," the narrator said. "The two brothers had many plans for the future, some involving commerce. But the young man had debts, gained from his own recklessness." Eerie music emerged from somewhere behind the stage curtains, a lone horn playing a soft melody. More horns joined the first and then drums entered the mix, raising in pitch and tempo.

The marionettes pranced about behind the white sheet, their shadows finally meeting one another at its center. The narrator intoned, "The young man betrayed his only brother, stealing much of his wealth and fleeing the city." With that, the marionettes whirled about, one smacking the other before rushing away. The horns and drums clamored, their notes dissonant and frantic.

The two figures behind the sheet vanished and were replaced by another set of marionettes, this time the outlines of a bride and her groom. The horns and drums played a somber wedding march, and the narrator continued his tale: "The young man soon after wed, the marriage rooted in false promises to his adored one. He then squandered the riches taken from his family, as well as most of what he and his new wife owned. She resisted, and he betrayed her."

The figure of the bride ran from the groom, but the groom figure caught her. The music of the horns and drums had grown loud and urgent, but now dropped suddenly into silence. The groom marionette struck the bride and she fell. The groom fled out of view. The shadow of the bride slowly rose and then backed away toward the edge of the white sheet, until she disappeared as well.

The narrator paused and the horns droned on flatly, setting a slow and bleak tone. "The young man had lost his love, but he only cared for coin," the narrator said, the timbre of his voice deeply melancholy. "And his profligate ways finally brought upon him the wrath of his lenders' henchmen." The horns and drums rose yet again, this time joined by a crashing cymbal: sharp, reverberating strikes again and again, and then nothing, the instruments falling silent all at once.

"The men of vengeance seized the young man to extort from him his unpaid debts," the narrator said, an immense sadness marking his words. The shadows of several marionettes depicting armed soldiers appeared and surrounded the marionette of the young man, who was once again at the center of the semitransparent sheet. The music of the horns and drums resumed, becoming chaotic as the mercenaries pulled their prisoner from sight.

Low horns played a sorrowful dirge, unpinning the story's final stretch. "The young man pleaded with them, begging for mercy, imploring clemency as he had just recently wed. Instead, the man was met with callous indifference as his captors meted out their final redress."

The solitary silhouette of a skeletal figure appeared behind the marionettes' sheet, grasping a scythe in its bony hands. "Death came for the young man," the narrator pronounced, "but not before great suffering. He would now forever be a part of the city, hidden within its gloomy depths." The sound of the horns faded, and the torches on stage grew dim as the amphitheater fell into darkness.

Ferdinando leaped to his feet and spun about, looking all around. The stage and the amphitheater were gone, replaced by an empty, debris-strewn lot walled in on all sides by rotting tenements. Glancing down, Ferdinando saw that he had been seated on a worn gravestone, the broken head of a winged cherub its sole remaining etching.

Only the winds softly whistling over the moonlight-struck tombstones could be heard now.

Down a dark tunnel, Ferdinando saw a jumble of lit torches leading away from the abandoned cemetery. He followed the bobbing lights as they descended, before emerging into the city's discarded and forgotten catacombs.

Ferdinando advanced through the winding and claustrophobic passageways beneath the city, twisting and turning in their cramped, lightless spaces, until he saw the torches stop somewhere in the darkness ahead. Stepping through an archway, he found the troupe from the shadow-play phantasmagoria standing watch over Ferdinando's street urchin guide, their dying torches smoldering in the stale air of the open crypt.

"It is here, *signore*. Here is where you were laid to rest." The urchin, paler and more cadaverous than before, pointed at a freshly bricked-up wall in the columbarium. Ferdinando paused and glimpsed row after row of moldering urns resting in stone recesses, the remains of generations long since deceased. His shaky memory now began to return to him, and he realized that he remembered this dismal place.

The phantom troupe members parted to make way as Ferdinando rushed to the site of his immurement, pressing his ear against the brickwork surface. Faint gasps could be heard, last breaths spent within the silence of the enclosed space. Ferdinando reeled back from the makeshift tomb, the events of the prior nights now flooding into his mind's eye.

"Please, I beg you. I can pay," Ferdinando shrieked, nearly stumbling with every step forward. "My brother will answer soon. I implore you, give me this last chance to pay my debt." Ferdinando struggled in the grasp of the two rough-looking men

in leathers who led him through the catacombs, their gauntlet-clad hands holding him firmly by the arms.

Two more condottiere walked behind Ferdinando and his twin escort, holding brightly burning torches aloft. At the front of the procession was an older man wearing an eye patch, accoutered in the colorful military garb of a Florentine officer.

The officer stepped under a stone archway, the shadows cast by the torches of his men stretching over the floor of the columbarium as they trod in after him. Ferdinando looked ahead and spied an open cavity in the wall of the crypt. Piles of bricks, masonry tools, and a bucket for mortar were laid out in front.

Ferdinando breathed a single panicked gulp as he realized what the mercenaries had planned for him. The Florentine stopped, grabbed Ferdinando by his face, and looked him in the eye before speaking.

"You are as worthless as you are dishonest, signore," he exclaimed, releasing Ferdinando's face in disgust. "We've held you for a fortnight and heard nothing from your family. No one cares to pay your debts. Your family and friends have disowned you, as you deserve."

With a gesture from the officer, the mercenaries pulled off Ferdinando's doublet and shoes, and then pushed him into the waiting alcove. One of the men held his sword to Ferdinando's throat as two others began to seal him into the catacombs, brick by brick.

Ferdinando sobbed as the final brick was cemented into place, blocking out the torchlight. Pressing against the cold wall of the tomb, Ferdinando wept in the darkness. How long would it take him to die?

Exhaling its last mortal breath, Ferdinando's body finally released his spirit. Ferdinando departed the catacombs to walk the streets of the city before dawn.

The streets and byways of the city were thronged with the spirits of the dead from all ages, always unseen by the living despite vastly outnumbering them. Ferdinando walked among the other spirits, some terrifying, many bearing the scars of their unfortunate deaths.

Victims of the plague, soldiers fallen in battle, murdered bawds and urchins, the old, the infirm, those who had succumbed to starvation, those who died violently through treachery, and those who'd suffered a whole litany of other gruesome deaths. As he roamed the streets that night, Ferdinando's ghost passed the house of his most beloved, held now and for all eternity behind the Veil of Memory.

Cast in Amber

The young shepherd held his torch high and peered expectantly into the surrounding darkness. He thought he'd heard a noise somewhere in the distance, but now only the deathly silence of the night greeted him. *What was that?* Costa thought, now alarmed. It had seemed like the cry of some animal, but he couldn't be certain.

He turned and slowly walked away from the cliff's sloping ledge. Ahead stretched the subtle trail of footprints left by his father and the hunting party, leading deep into the cave. The band of men had tracked the wolves for several days to what they believed was their lair, but this cave seemed to be something else. What was once a natural cavern had been recast into a kind of hypogeum, with ghastly totems of carnage set on either side of its entrance. *Who could have put such a warning here? Surely not the wolves,* Costa thought as he scrutinized the totems, shivering slightly in the cool nighttime air.

There were sudden cries, as if the men had been startled, their astonished gasps echoing from the cavern below. Costa heard his father as he strode forward to investigate: "Costa, remain on your guard!" A pause. Then: "It's nothing, only a picture on the wall."

Obeying his father without a word, Costa climbed back to the dusty, flat plateau that met the cave's mouth and resumed his watch. He made a final glance at the entrance totems. They were fashioned from human skulls, any flesh long since stripped bare. Shuddering involuntarily, Costa again gazed out into the hushed night and the stark wilderness around him, its mass of tortured oaks and twisted brambles abutting the foot of the cave's barren hill.

Now that he was sure his son was at his station, Rufus returned his attention to the strange mural. Under the light of their torches, he and the other shepherds studied the daubed ochre rendering of a she-wolf suckling her two cubs. The painting was large, sprawling across the wall of the cave. What had shocked Rufus and his men was the strikingly lifelike depiction of the mural's cubs, portrayed as a disturbing mélange of wolf and human child, their eyes feral but keen, their paws almost like hands.

"There is much more to this wolf-pack than we suspected," Rufus said, fear creeping into his voice as he looked over the grim faces at his side. "These are not ordinary wolves, but profane spirits, cursed by the gods for some terrible crime. Stephanus spoke the truth when he said these beasts can assume the form of men."

Stepping away from the wall painting, Rufus pointed onward. "We must be quick. Aurelia may be somewhere in the cave."

The party followed Rufus deeper into the tenebrous passageway, making fleeting glances at the mural as they filed past. As they descended into depths of the cavern, the band's waning torches cast gigantic shadows, exaggerated imitations of the cave's hanging stalactites, protruding rock formations, and the men's own proportions.

From among the villagers Rufus had chosen four men and his elder son for his hunting party. Their steadings had been beset by a pack of roaming wolves and, while the attacks had lasted less than a fortnight, the loss of livestock was all but unbearable. Their village was isolated from the larger towns and cities; the provincial authorities in the distant capital were too far removed to be reached in time. The final attack ended with one shepherd's daughter being carried off by the wolves, taken from her bed as she slept.

Aurelia's father, Caius, unexpectedly halted, stopping the party in its tracks. "Did you hear that?" he said to his fellows, his voice strained and urgent as he choked out the words. "There's a girl sobbing, somewhere ahead. That's my daughter. My Aurelia!"

The men listened, but all that was audible was the distant sound of dripping water monotonously tapping against stone. In a panic, Caius pushed past Rufus and another shepherd, rushing forward into the darkness of the cave, his torch held out before him. Caius fell with a clatter and disappeared, crying out as the light from his torch was abruptly extinguished.

Shouting down into the cave's passage, Rufus exclaimed, "Caius, you fool, you've put us all in danger!" He then scoured the blackness with his torch but failed to see where Caius had fallen. Rufus turned to his men, hastily instructing them: "Go grab him, and then let's search for any sign of Aurelia. Caius couldn't have gotten too far ahead."

Rufus had only taken a few steps before he noticed two sets of glowing red eyes watching the men intently from the cave's gloaming recesses. Under flickering torchlight, the faint outline of an enormous wolf's head appeared, with a second wolf of similar size trailing not far behind it.

The first wolf leaped as Rufus drew his *gladius* from his belt, a relic from his time in the legion. The shepherd before Rufus was taken down with a piercing scream, the massive wolf tearing the man's throat out with one quick laceration from its jaws. Rufus spun, finding several more sets of glinting lupine eyes propagating around him in the shadows.

Rufus thrust with his *gladius*, stabbing deeply into a charging wolf. Howling, the beast fell aside. Rufus dropped his sputtering torch and bolted past its bleeding carcass. Two wolves gave chase, but Rufus's aged yet sturdy legs sped him forward. The dying shrieks of his men rang out from the cavern walls as they were torn to gory shreds, the victims of yet more wolves.

Tumbling out onto the hill's rocky plateau, Rufus nearly stumbled over the mutilated body of his son, the boy's dead eyes staring up into the night's starry heavens. The wolves continued to pursue their quarry, loping down through the brush surrounding the sloping hill and then out into the open fields spanning it, the waving grasses trampled beneath Rufus's sandaled feet.

As he ran, Rufus rapidly scanned the moonlit horizon for somewhere to climb, anywhere the wolves might not reach him. Not far ahead was a hillside cluster of sparsely distributed trees near an outcropping of jutting rocks.

Scaling the trunk of a sagging oak, Rufus pulled himself onto its generous bough and lay, arms clutching the wide branch. He crawled along its length, reaching a spot at its middle, near the craggy cliffs of the hill. Rufus checked his belt and realized he had dropped his *gladius* as he'd fled the caves.

The howls of the wolf pack grew nearer as they closed in on his hillside hiding place. Out the corner of his eye, Rufus spied the shape of a huge wolf perched on a cliff facing his tree branch. The wolf pounced just as Rufus tried to roll away, ripping him from the branches of the oak and onto the ground below. Rufus was silent as he met his death in the slavering jaws of the black wolf, a stoic soldier until the end.

Dragging the mangled corpse of the hunting party's leader behind it, the black-furred wolf returned to its pack. The alpha dropped Rufus's savaged remains onto the cave floor, where it lay surrounded by the gnawed and littered bones of the wolf pack's prey, both man and animal.

The wolf stretched out onto its forepaws before its assembled packmates, almost fluidly metamorphosing into a man. A teenage girl sat before a great gray wolf crouching on its haunches, her plain linen tunic torn and disheveled as she looked on.

The man rose from the cave floor and brought the girl to her bare feet, wrapping her in his sinewy arms in a perverse embrace. At first caressing the girl's neck, his bloody hand came to rest upon her shoulder as he began to speak to his brethren: "Soon, there will be new cubs," the man said, his voice a low and menacing growl. "The pack will swell in number. The usurpers will then know fear, as did our forebearers who were laid to waste before them."

Wild-eyed and filthy, the girl tittered insanely as the pack leader finished his vow, her mind mostly gone. The man turned her to face him, leaning down to meet the girl's parched lips and kissing her deeply on the mouth. The wolf pack howled in unison, a chilling howl of vengeance, their call reverberating off the blood-drenched walls of the wolf den and echoing out into the desolate night.

Appius and Lucius sat idly beside each other on a bench in the provincial governor's villa, one of many carved marble benches in the lengthy hallway. They rested in the shade of the villa's columnated front entrance, finding their seat cool to the touch despite the hot day outside.

Stirring for a moment, Lucius peered down the empty hallway. At the end of the row of benches was a statue of the emperor in military dress, the unoccupied space's only guardian. At once both regal and ascendant, the emperor's likeness conveyed a spirit of triumph after many hard-won victories. His uncle, Lucius noticed, was nodding off, but started when a young attendant appeared at his side.

"This way, please. The proconsul will see you now," the attendant said stiffly, walking quickly ahead and not bothering to note whether he was being followed. The travel-weary twosome trudged after the youth, who soon stopped in front of an open archway. "Here. Someone will return for you after your meeting with the proconsul." Unsmiling, the attendant then strode off, failing to make eye contact with either of his charges even once.

Appius glanced over at his nephew as they stood before the archway. "Big city manners," he said, shrugging wryly. Then, gesturing forward, he said, "You lead the way, Lucius. Proconsul Drusus hasn't seen you since you were a child."

Lucius stepped into the proconsul's official chambers, an open, spacious office featuring shelf after shelf of bound scrolls along its brightly painted walls. The arched and glassless windows of the chamber provided a picturesque view of the capital's calm seaside harbor and the azure summer sky under which it was sheltered. A stern-looking older man, robed in the long tunic and *pallium* of his position, turned to greet the visitors as Lucius drew near, Appius at his side.

"So, this is Rufus Norbanus' younger son, Lucius," the man said, at first seeming dispassionate but then breaking into a broad smile, the creases around his eyes stretching to his graying temples. "Come," the proconsul said as he looked over Lucius, "sit here and let's catch up on what the family has been doing out on the estates."

Proconsul Publius Claudius Drusus embraced Appius by clasping both the man's muscular forearms before resting on a reclining couch near his desk, offering the remaining two seats to Appius and Lucius.

"I'm afraid I am the bearer of bad news, Publius Drusus," Appius explained, somber as he braced himself for what was to come. "My brother, Rufus Flaccus, is dead, as is his elder son and my nephew, Costa. They were slain in the pursuit of a girl from our village who had been taken by a pack of wolves. None in the hunting party had returned after more than a week, so we have assumed the worst." Appius studied Publius Drusus's austere, aquiline face, worried that even Rufus's former commander might be shattered after learning about the death of his old friend.

Publius sat in silence as Rufus finished speaking. "Are you sure, Appius?" he said slowly, stunned. "You have nothing but a prolonged absence to confirm their deaths?" Publius had become visibly crestfallen, an abrupt change from his almost buoyant demeanor just moments ago.

"The council of elders debated sending a rescue party, but the howls of the wolves were heard outside the village soon after," Appius replied, feeling a slight chill upon recalling that night's rapacious howling. "If Rufus and his men had found the wolf den, either they would have slain the wolves, or the wolves killed them. The hunter, Quintus, was with the party and he could track a beast to the ends of the world. They surely found what they were looking for."

Publius stood and walked to an open window, his hands meeting behind his back. Gazing out past the sheer cliffs at the villa's periphery, he said, "So that is why you are here? To ask for my intervention?"

Appius arose from his seat. "Yes, Proconsul, we ask that you send a *centuria* from your garrison to deal with these predators once and for all. We request Marcus Arcturus as the centurion, a good friend of both Rufus Flaccus and myself." Appius uttered these words directly and firmly, knowing this was likely the only chance he and his people had to save themselves.

"So many men, Appius! How could you need that many legionaries?" Publius said as he turned to face Appius, his face betraying his sadness and incredulity.

Having said almost nothing during the conversation, Lucius suddenly interrupted, his voice taut and urgent: "These are not just wolves, Proconsul Drusus. These are the malign spirits of the dead who have come upon us, driven by a vendetta against the living. My belief is that they are the *Etruscī*, returned to despoil the lands taken from them by our ancestors. But they are yet flesh and blood and can be returned to the netherworld with a sword."

Publius' heavy brow furrowed, his face now appearing almost angry instead of despondent. "Those tales of the *Etruscī* are nothing but superstition, stories to frighten unruly children," he said, the scornful annoyance in his tone evident as he waved his hand. "Wolves have preyed upon the province's herds for generations, but they are just that: wolves. Merely common beasts impelled by the need to eat and to survive." Publius turned to Appius as if for support, but was met instead by morose silence.

"I beg your pardon, Proconsul," Lucius said at last. "We have as witness one of the most trusted men in our village. He swore these wolves can walk on two legs after taking the shape of men. What he saw one night nearly sent him to Orcus." Lucius breathed in and then gulped before continuing, halfway stricken by fear as he began to retell Stephanus' story.

"Stephanus, the village cartwright and a respected elder, was on his smallholding after the attacks first began. He was outside securing his shed against the depredations of the wolves; valuables had been found missing from the village after the attacks. How mere wolves could steal coin and belongings wasn't clear, but it soon became so.

"As Stephanus barred the shed door, he spied the silhouettes of several wolves in the moonlight. They began prowling up the path to his family's villa. Stephanus stopped and hid behind the shed, not wanting to draw their attention. His wife and children had left to stay with his wife's sister in a neighboring village the day before, so the house was now unoccupied.

"Once the wolf pack reached the entrance, they began to transform, shifting and taking on new shapes. Without so much as a sound, the strange beasts assumed human form and stood upright, unclothed and unshorn. The bare, shaggy men then forced open the villa's front door, breaking the lock with only their brute strength.

"The bandits piled in and soon emerged holding a bulging sack, which was then strapped to the backs of one of the men. The house thieves fell to their knees and regained the bodies of monstrous wolves, metamorphosing in mere moments. The pack gathered and let out a blood-curdling victory howl before disappearing into the night, the clanging of Stephanus's stolen silverware ringing behind them as they fled."

Lucius paused his narrative and eyed Publius' face, but the older man gave nothing away. "Well, Stephanus was petrified in his hiding place, trembling in terror, now certain our little community had somehow brought the fury of the gods down upon us. He prayed to Lupercus that what he had seen was only a trick of a frightened mind, but in his heart he knew otherwise."

Publius studied Lucius for a moment and then moved to seat himself behind his desk. Speaking forthrightly to both men, Publius said, "I will make an offering at the temple to Apollo this evening and let the divinity speak to me through the sibyl. You will have my answer in the morning once I have pondered the sibyl's riddle. An attendant will now show you to your rooms."

Indicating an end to their meeting, Publius Drusus stood once again and turned to look out the window at the midday sun reflecting off the sparkling waters of the harbor. Appius and Lucius stepped into the hallway, finding a second attendant waiting for them. They were led across the villa's sprawling courtyard, itself lined with shrubbery and marble statuary and with a flowing fountain at its center. The attendant paused at a suite of rooms facing the courtyard and opened its door for the guests.

"So, this is where they put our satchels," Appius observed as he reached down to search their luggage. "I was worried someone had run off with them."

"What do you think?" Lucius said, an authentic bewilderment hanging over him as he sat on his mattress and watched Appius unpack. "Will Proconsul Drusus help us?"

"I believe so," Appius assured him, digging through a small leather *loculus* as he spoke. "Publius' belief in the gods is not strong, but he may listen to the oracle. My own opinion is that Publius may just be looking for a scapegoat, pinning the decision to deploy troops to the outlands on the sibyl's prattle instead of on himself."

"You don't believe in the gods, do you, Appius?" Lucius seemed almost surprised as he asked the question to his uncle.

"I believe in our family, our village, and our safety, Lucius," Appius replied matter-of-factly. "My brother and my nephew are dead, as are several other villagers. If Publius must burn some incense or 'sacrifice' nine *popona* to save us from the wolves then so be it."

"I'm going to visit the villa baths before the *cena*," Lucius said, quickly burying the subject at hand. "I'm dusty after our long journey. I just hope Proconsul Drusus didn't notice."

Lucius left the guest rooms to walk to the baths, excited to indulge in such a modern convenience. He thought back to their meeting with Publius Drusus and how the proconsul had seemed almost afraid to admit the wolves might be the vengeful spirits of the *Etruscī*.

Publius Drusus, Appius, his own father, and Marcus Arcturus had all served together in the legion, stationed at what was then the far-flung edge of the Empire. *Is there something about the wolves Appius and Publius Drusus know but are not admitting?* Lucius mused as he entered the villa's *caldarium*, the heated room's hot, moist air quickly opening the pores of his dry skin. Lucius sat to remove his worn sandals and then quietly prayed, hoping his father's old friend would send aid before it was too late.

The late afternoon sun bore down on Appius and Lucius' horse-drawn cart as it entered the village's main thoroughfare, the men exhausted after their days-long journey. The villagers had been roused by the loud clacking of iron-shod wheels over the westerly hills and emerged from their simple dwellings along the wide road to watch the travelers' return.

An older man followed by a great, heavily-jowled dog opened the door to his home and approached the cart as it slowly rolled past. The dog accompanying the man bore fresh scars across its nose and cheek, evidence of the most recent wolf attack.

"*Salvē*, Appius Flaccus. Do you bring good news or bad news back with you? I pray your time with the proconsul was not wasted."

Appius drew the cart to a gradual stop, and the man reached up to put a brawny hand on his shoulder before Appius could even answer him.

"A full *centuria* will arrive in less than half a fortnight, Atticus," Appius announced, with no small measure of enthusiasm despite his weariness. "And Marcus Arcturus will lead them. The wolves will meet their end when they harass us again."

"Excellent, Appius!" Atticus said, patting Appius' shoulder in thanks. "The legion will deal with this menace. We must prepare a temporary barracks for the men before their arrival." Atticus then strode off to converse with the villagers who had gathered nearby, his guard dog in tow.

Appius urged his cart horse down to where the main road ended, finally branching off into the outlying farmsteads. His family's small villa was on the village outskirts, with its own plot of land—it had been bequeathed to Rufus Flaccus as payment for his services to the legion. Lucius now lived with his aunt, uncle, and their children in the villa, his father and brother gone. Lucius's mother had died years before.

Lucius removed his wide-brimmed hat, hung it up, and undid the brooch holding his drab *lacerna*. His travel clothes would be stored away after laundering, he hoped for the foreseeable future. Appius was greeted by his wife, Aelia, and his children, who told him a supper had been prepared for their coming. After supper, Lucius and Appius sat outside on wood *sella* taken from the kitchen, watching a burnt orange sun set over the hills they had just traveled.

"I explored many lands in my youth as part of the legion," Appius said, breaking an uncomfortable silence after the sun had disappeared behind the hills. "But I'm sure your father must have told you some of our stories. Publius Drusus and Marcus Arcturus were valiant men, stalwarts against the *Germani* and other barbarous adversaries. Why, I remember this one time, we—"

"Father never spoke to us about his time in the legion," Lucius said suddenly, his gaze still fixed on the now-dark horizon. "He was proud of his service, but the killing... it never sat well with him. I think he was afraid he'd become used to it." Lucius looked over at Appius, unsure whether Rufus had revealed such anxieties to his younger brother.

"Rufus never flinched. He met death head-on and spit in its face. I'm sure that's how he met his end with the wolves." Appius smiled slightly as he spoke, as if recalling some act of bravery. "He must have taken a wolf or two with him."

Lucius leaned back on his stool and rested his brow in his hand. "Father did tell us one story about his coming home after a long campaign," Lucius finally said after a lengthy pause. "He probably told it to us as the story was so peculiar. You were with him if I remember correctly."

"Aye, I might recall it. Did the story involve a woman? A woman and her two sons?"

"That's the one," Lucius confirmed. "Marcus Arcturus had allowed his men to break ranks after the long campaign and leave with their own *contubernia* instead of waiting with the rest of the legion. The discharged *contubernales* passed near the borderlands of the Empire on the way home to their families.

"Even though Father was their *decanus*, you and Father broke from the other men returning home, all of them eager to see loved ones. Off from the roadside was a thatched cottage, partially hidden by the dense woods."

Appius agreed, seeming to recall more of the story now. "That's it. A strange old woman lived in that hut, half-mad, I think. But what else did your father tell you about her?"

"That she invited you in, both of you, and bid you stay the night," Lucius replied, a moment of clarity coming upon him. "She told you her own story, one about the wolves that roamed the black forestlands. She sat you next to the fire, gave you something to eat, and then began her odd tale..."

Rufus put aside his wooden spoon and began sopping up the last remnants of gruel with a thick slice of dark bread. He and Appius had eaten only early that morning and it was now close to sunset. The compatriots were tired after their long trek across the borderlands, having made most of the journey on foot. When they had spied a lonely cottage at the woodland boundary, they immediately sought shelter within.

"Gratias tibi. *We appreciate your hospitality,*" Rufus said as he watched the woman and Appius eating, the three of them having dined in polite silence until that moment. The trio sat around a smoldering firepit, the fire's charcoal-colored smoke drifting up through a blackened hole in the straw roof of the cottage. "We're still a long way from our village," Rufus continued amicably. "This is what the imperial subjects in Aegyptus might call an 'oasis' along our journey home."

"I have little company, and you men are both in the legion. Think nothing of it," the woman replied casually, finishing with her meal and setting her bowl aside. She stood and took the men's bowls and her own to a washing basin laid on the cottage's earthen floor. Rufus observed her movements as she cleaned up, guessing her weathered appearance hid her actual age. She may even have been quite beautiful at one time, not so long ago.

"You had better check your pack mule," the woman said as she washed. "It could be a long night. The forest's edge is not safe, but I live here nonetheless."

"What's your name, woman?" Appius asked abruptly, having been quiet since taking his seat by the fire. "You've invited us in for the night, but we still don't know your name."

"I am Servilia," the woman replied, almost bothered by the question. "These lands are not my native lands, and the people who dwell past this forest are not my kin."

"I am Appius Flaccus, and this is my older brother, Rufus Flaccus," Appius said, with Rufus nodding briefly as he was introduced. "Our families are waiting for us farther along, and we hope to return to them safely. Once we have slept, we'll be on our way again in the morning."

A lone wolf howled somewhere out in the forest. Servilia looked toward the crude door of the one-room cottage and then back down at the basin, as if hoping the unsettling call would go unmentioned.

"I'll go check on our mule," said Rufus. "She could use more feed grass if we sleep past sunrise." He stood and began striding toward the cottage door, wondering why their host had ignored the sound of imminent danger not so far away.

"Wait, please. Don't venture outside just yet," Servilia pleaded, holding an outstretched hand toward Rufus. "I must tell you a story first, to help you understand why I am here, alone in these woods." Servilia gestured for Rufus to sit again by the fire, its flickering light casting shadows over her creased, weather-beaten face. "My time may soon end, and I need to pass something on to you before you take your leave of me."

Appius glanced over at his brother as Rufus took his seat on one of several decrepit wooden stools placed around the firepit. Servilia then reached under her mottled tunic to produce a silver-white coin hanging from a chain around her neck. The coin shone brightly as Servilia dangled the pendant near the light of the fire, its gleaming, argent surface in sharp contrast to the cottage's colorless, dingy interior.

"This amulet was forged in Hispania," she murmured, as if dragging forward distant memories. "It has protected me in this desolate place from what lurks at night in the forest."

Servilia then closed her hand around the pendant, suddenly breaking what was almost a hypnotic moment. Rufus and Appius were now very quiet, both feeling there was much more to this beggarly woman than they had first believed.

"I met him at the festival of the Lupercalia when I was only a girl. A man appeared in the crowd wearing the mask of the wolf. He took me and loved me. Soon after, I found I was with child—twins. The children were born in secret, away from my family, as there was no father.

"I raised my two sons alone, not far from this comfortless abode I now call my home. They grew to early manhood, and that is when the bloodlust came upon them. One day, I returned home late from the market to find two wolves, distinct from each other by the color of their coats. That this had occurred was impossible, but I knew they were my sons."

Servilia stared into the fire, lost for a moment but then flaring with sudden determination. "My sons had slaughtered our small flock of sheep in their pen. They were feeding on the carcasses when I interrupted them. One appeared ready to pounce, but the other howled into the twilight, impelling both to flee. Since that day, my sons have led the wolf packs in the hills and forests of this forsaken land."

Without pausing to mark a conclusion to the story, Servilia stood and walked to the cottage wall facing the firepit, over which hung a tattered cloth. She pulled the cloth down from its hooks to display a painting, one stained into the daub itself. It was a coarse yet vivid depiction of a she-wolf suckling two cubs, her offspring demonic and half-human in appearance.

"These demi-human beasts are cursed by the gods, avatars of revenge and depraved appetites," Servilia declared as she stood before the painting, holding forth the silver pendant. "These creatures call themselves 'the Children of Lupercus,' but they are nothing of the sort. They are infernal, and spring from the underworld itself."

Servilia stepped back toward the firepit and held the pendant before Rufus, letting it drop into his open palm. Rufus could now see the image engraved into the metal. It was much like that of the wall painting: a mother wolf with her two whelps.

"The amulet is blessed," Servilia continued vehemently, nearly shaking as she spoke, "and can seal the curse of the Luperci, trapping it in a moment of time as a moth might be cast in amber. The amulet can also act as a ward, protecting those threatened by the demons' fangs and claws."

With that, Servilia turned and let out a hacking cough, steadying herself against the wall as she did so. Facing them again, Servilia whispered, "My time is short, and they know it. The wolves close in on me. I will be too weak to use the amulet when they finally come."

Lucius turned to look at Appius in the faint moonlight, pausing the retelling of his father's story. "And then the three of you bed down to sleep, the woman's wheezing breaths soon growing shallow as she lay nearby. You and

Father conspired to slip away, fearful not only that she was mad, but that she might carry the pestilence."

Stunned by the sharpness of Lucius's memory, Appius only nodded. He then said, "As we left in the dead of night, many eyes appeared outside the hut, watching us from the fringes of the forest. The wolves let us pass unmolested on the empty road, receding into the distance as we took the path home. As for what became of the woman...well. It's best not to dwell upon it."

"Where did you find it?" Appius asked, studying the silver pendant that swayed gently in his grasp. He recognized the relief of the she-wolf and cubs engraved into its coin.

"In a little box, among Father's personal belongings," Lucius replied, satisfied that he'd been able to recover this lost possession. "Father was very private and kept things from his days in the legion hidden away in a chest. I would have never found it if Father were still with us." More quietly, he added, "Father may have forgotten about the amulet. It might have saved him."

"That woman was mad, Lucius," Appius scoffed. "How she came upon such a fine piece of jewelry is the only unexplainable thing from her ravings. She was destitute in that shack out in the woods."

Lucius took the pendant back from Appius. "The old woman told you this amulet was blessed. By whom, I wonder?" He looped the pendant's chain around his neck and tucked its coin under his tunic.

"The priests of Lupercus, the *Luperci*? Who knows, some divinity. I believe none of it." Appius shrugged dismissively.

"Some say that Lupercus is really Faunus," Lucius noted. "The horned god of the forest. He also relishes in playing tricks on mortals, or so it is said."

"Again, nonsense. Come, let's be about it." Appius pushed open the front door to their villa and handed Lucius a heavy *pilum*, its iron point recently sharpened. Fastening his *gladius* to his belt, Appius then led Lucius down the road to the village.

It was early evening. The howling of the wolves had kept many in the village awake the previous night, and all felt better having Marcus Arcturus and the men of his *centuria* around. They had arrived that morning and were busy preparing for the return of the wolf pack.

"*Salvē*, Marcus Arcturus. Are your men ready at their stations? The wolves attacked our people in their homes when they last came upon us." Appius embraced the imposing man in centurion's uniform as they stood at the village road's center. The man's raven hair was streaked with gray, his face marred from many long campaigns.

"We await the wolves. Forty men are sequestered in your village hall and will emerge in force once the pack begins its predations. Our war hounds are with them, collared and set." Marcus Arcturus then nodded to Lucius, acknowledging the son of his best soldier and close friend.

"Excellent. Thank you, especially for sending men to family households. Four of your men are at our villa now. Should the wolves enter, they will surely be surprised." Appius smiled broadly as he said this, hopeful that the moment of revenge was at hand.

The sun began to disappear behind the hills surrounding the village. An uneasy quiet descended, as if all knew something terrible was about to happen but none dared speak of it aloud.

Appius and Lucius sat at the dining table with Atticus and his wife, Atticus's big dog resting at their feet.

DOORWAYS TO THE UNSEEN 3

"Your house is near the middle thoroughfare, Atticus. If the wolves come upon the road, we can rush to them and attack." Appius unconsciously put his hand over his belt as he said this, seeking the assurance his battle-worn *gladius* provided him.

A solitary wolf howl pierced the night. Distant, yes, but soon joined by a cacophony of howls much closer. Appius arose from his seat at the table just as the front door burst in violently, a sable black wolf leaping to meet his throat, the broken door falling aside.

The wolf thrashed Appius's limp body back and forth across the wooden table, blood coating the walls as Lucius reached for his *pilum*. The wolf dropped Appius from its jaws and then turned to Lucius and Atticus, finding both men armed and ready.

Baring its fangs ferociously, the wolf leaped aside as Lucius jabbed with his *pilum*. Swinging his club, Atticus was blocked by another wolf which had darted in from the village thoroughfare, the road outside now swarming with wolves of varying sizes and rustic hues.

Atticus fell under the second wolf's assault, his guard dog yowling as it was mobbed by more wolves and then brought down. Escaping through the open doorway to the road, Lucius saw what was happening: dozens, perhaps over a hundred wolves were swarming into the village, crashing against a wall of legionaries, war dogs, and armed villagers.

A soldier close to Lucius cried out as he was leaped upon by two wolves and pulled down, his *scutum* and *gladius* falling from his hands. Lucius turned and was met by an enormous auburn wolf, crouched, blood and saliva dripping from its jaws.

The wolf's great forepaws met Lucius's chest just as he reached under his tunic, knocking him back. Lucius struggled under its crushing weight, the beast's overpowering scent being almost too much to bear. With all the strength he could muster, Lucius managed to pull forth the hidden pendant with his free hand.

The pendant's coin glowed eerily with an otherworldly blue aura. The wolf recoiled and wailed, convulsing in a pantomime of excruciating pain as it fell back and then fled into the tumultuous throng around them. Recovering, Lucius pulled himself to his feet and surveyed the ongoing fray.

Bodies were strewn everywhere: some wolves, but mostly the men and dogs who had fought against them. The remaining legionaries had formed a tight circle with their *scuta* facing outward, stabbing at charging wolves attempting to break their ranks. Lucius turned and ran down the road to his family's villa, fearful his only remaining kin might also be dead.

The villa door was broken when he arrived, a bloody trail on the antechamber's floor leading away from the entrance. Lucius gripped his *pilum* with both hands and cautiously stepped into the darkened entryway. He soon found a pair of soldiers, torn and lacerated, as well as a slain wolf in the hall to the kitchen. Waves of splattered blood adorned the hallway's domestic fresco.

A low growl rumbled in the passage behind Lucius. He turned and was confronted by a sleek gray wolf a few paces away, a prominent sword gash splitting its bloodied muzzle.

The beast tensed, about to leap, just as the eerie blue light of the pendant swelled again. The wolf yelped, the sound almost pitiful, and raced away. Lucius watched it go before continuing his search. Before long, he found his aunt and the two remaining legionaries dead on the villa grounds outside.

Where are the children? Lucius thought, almost sure the wolves had taken them. His two young cousins, the daughters of Appius and Aelia, were nowhere to be seen. The villa seemed deserted now, otherwise silent save for the sounds of fighting between men and wolves, ambient in the distance. Searching further, Lucius found a torn piece of a tunic and one of the girls' loose sandals. Neither had blood on them.

The argent coin hanging from its chain glowed more brightly than ever before at this unexpected discovery, as if the pendant were attempting to lead Lucius to the girls' wolfish abductors. Lucius wandered into the night, following the faraway howling, the pendant pulling him forward.

He stumbled in the dark, the waning moon providing little illumination as he reached the low hills outside the village, trusting in pendant that shone like a floating beacon in an ocean of darkness. Soon, Lucius reached the encampment of the wolves. There, half a dozen of them lay licking their wounds around two prisoners.

The kidnapped cousins were bound and gagged, and lay resting against several sacks of stolen goods. The elder of the two girls, Norbana, saw Lucius approaching and began to struggle against her bonds, her muffled cries alerting the injured wolf pack.

Lucius strode boldly into the camp's center as the wolves arose, the pendant now blazing with a brilliant white-blue light. The wolfen creatures shrieked and howled, several limping away into the surrounding darkness, others falling and convulsing in the mud. Only one wolf, a great black beast, remained to face Lucius.

The enormous black wolf stood on its hind legs and began to reshape itself into a naked man, his ebon-hued hair matted with blood, as had been the wolf's coat. The alpha wolf, the surviving son of Servilia, reached for his blade.

"I shall kill you as a man, worthless cur," he spat, his voice harsh and venomous. "It's what one such as you deserve."

The man darted forward, slashing viciously with his curved dagger, narrowing missing Lucius's arms and throat. Lucius quickly stepped back and held the argent coin high, its unearthly bluish rays now coalescing into a loping wolf pack, translucent and ghostly in its aspect.

The celestial wolves descended from the night sky along an invisible path and thronged the man, dragging him screaming down into the earth, into the chthonian underworld of Pluto.

Lucius kept his *pilum* poised, ready for another attack, but as the moments passed in silence, he realized the daemon wolf had been cast out from this world by the noble spirits of the wolves he and his packmates had corrupted. The night on the hills was still, save for the frightened weeping of Lucius's cousins.

He reached down into the dust to pick up the pendant, having dropped it as the wolf-wraiths descended. The argent coin gleamed in the moonlight, a fresh lupine soul trapped forever within, the curse of the *Luperci* bonded with the coin's alloy.

"Mere years ago, all of this was but uncultivated land for a thousand paces," Lucius enthused to the slim, smartly dressed man at his side who nodded, listening intently to his host. "My laborers and I have turned this plot into a thriving olive orchard, one which sells its produce as far away as the capital. My father never thought it was possible, but we did it." Lucius leaned on the villa balcony's balustrade, smiling at the wealthy merchant.

"I remember when your town was but a village, known mostly for its rocky soil," the man remarked blithely, his tone relaxed and casual. "You're right; what you've done here is a miracle, Lucius Flaccus, blessed by the gods." The merchant then drank from his cup, looking out from the balcony at the horizon as the summer sun dipped behind the hills. It would be nighttime soon.

"Yes, blessed by the gods. As you say." Lucius suddenly seemed absent-minded, as if recollecting a past tragedy that still haunted him. Lucius then smiled again, worried his guest might notice this fleeting moment of painful distraction.

"But it grows late, Gaius Polybius," he said swiftly, pulling himself back into the present. "My wife and one of our servants will show you to your rooms. Tomorrow we will draw up the contracts and complete the sale. *Bene quiescere.*"

The merchant nodded, bade Lucius goodnight, and stepped inside. Lucius turned back to peer out at the hills beyond. The marble balcony was one of his recent additions to his family's villa—an indulgence during this time of prosperity. Years had passed since the wolves had been driven from the village, the packs abruptly fleeing just as their victory over the legionaries appeared certain. They never returned.

The full moon was ripe and loomed large overhead as a warm breeze drifted over Lucius, helping to soothe his apprehension. Squinting into the darkness, Lucius thought he saw several shapes approaching from the road. They looked like animals, but he couldn't be sure.

Lucius kept the silver pendant in a ceramic urn high on a shelf in his bedroom, where his children couldn't reach it. His wife never inquired about the pendant, assuming it was some heirloom left to him by his father. Cursed, Lucius hoped the pendant would remain at the bottom of the urn for the rest of his days.

The wolves closed in, their sharp eyes shining in the dark, soon to reach the villa's front door.

Deep in the shaded urn, the pendant began to glow. The souls of the departed had returned, ready to take back their master's talisman.

Cabin in the Woods

There was a loud knock on the cabin door. Several more followed in rapid succession. The knocking was insistent, of someone desperate, or even of someone in imminent danger. All at once, it stopped.

Bleary-eyed and half-asleep, Howard pushed himself up from his fireside reading chair and put his ear to the door's solid wood. He waited for some sign, anything that might hint at the nature of the trespasser, but Howard heard nothing from the other side, only the crackling fire and the faint popping of burning wood behind him.

Stepping away, Howard dimly wondered who would be out on such a cold night. He hadn't seen anyone since the snowstorm.

He drew aside the curtain draping a frost-tinted window and peered into the winter night enveloping the cabin. A man wearing a bulky hooded coat stood alone at the door's threshold, arms limp, making no effort to knock again. The man neither turned his head nor looked down, instead staring forward at the door itself.

Howard grabbed his hunting rifle from its rack above the fireplace. Returning to the door, he called out to the unwanted visitor in an intimidating voice, "Whoever you are, you should go away. If you need help, my neighbor is back down the road. I can't let a perfect stranger in this late at night. Just go."

The stranger offered no reply, even as Howard removed the pivot safety from his rifle with its characteristic and very audible "clack" sound. Howard returned to the front window and pulled its curtain aside again. The man was gone.

Where could he have come from? Howard pondered. *The road's impassable. He couldn't have just walked here from town.*

Despite his better judgment, Howard unlocked the cabin door and slowly opened it, overcome by a disquieting curiosity. His rifle was ready in his other hand. The night outside was frigid, a gusting, arctic wind rustling the spruce trees that lined the path from the distant road. Howard stepped outside into the cold and the dark, the vapor of his breath instantly icy.

The lambent moon provided some visibility, its soft rays reflecting cleanly off the mounds of virgin snow piled high about the cabin. The snow crunched under Howard's boots as he paced around his wilderness home. The last snowfall had been comparatively light and he could actually walk outside unimpeded, which was unusual.

Howard found the man in the heavy coat lying face down in a snowbank near the cabin's tarpaulin-covered wood pile. Motionless, the man's arms were sprawled above his head. Quickly propping his rifle against the side of the cabin, Howard rushed to the fallen man, seizing him by the shoulder to turn him over.

The stranger appeared young and was bearded, strands of matted hair falling from under his parka's hood. His eyes shut, the man tilted his head and then coughed weakly.

"Can you hear me?" Howard inquired sharply, his legs half-buried in the snowbank. The man remained senseless. "What's your name?"

At this second question, the stranger opened his eyes, giving Howard a dull, uncomprehending stare.

Howard began to pull the man to his feet, shivering in the cold—he had failed to don a coat before stepping out. The man stumbled and nearly fell again, but Howard helped him to the cabin door, first taking his rifle from where he had left it.

Blustering winds from the freezing night swept into the cabin before Howard closed the door tightly behind them. He sat the man in a chair near the blazing fireplace, its embers sparking as Howard threw in more wood. While Howard mounted his rifle, the man reclined and looked about the room, seeming to come to his senses as the warmth of the cabin's interior revived him in some measure.

"Do you know where you are?" Howard asked, looking down at the man in his over-stuffed chair. "Again, what's your name?"

Towering shadows were thrown about the otherwise unlit room from the cabin's fireplace, with Howard's aging, craggy face somewhat softened by the fireplace's ruddy glow.

The man finally answered in a broken, halting voice, speaking as if he hadn't formed words for some time. "Do you... have... anything to drink? Water? Some... warm broth, maybe? Or... anything?" He pulled back the hood of his parka with a mittened hand and wiped his wet face as Howard turned away from him, taking a pot from a cupboard in the open room's small kitchen.

"I'll heat some broth for you," Howard called over his shoulder. "It'll be ready in a minute or two. You're my first caller since before the winter." Howard opened a can from the cupboard and poured broth into a lidless pot, covering it as the stove's burner ignited. Howard then sat in the other plush, upholstered chair before the fireplace and, for the first time, took a good look at his visitor.

The young man was handsome but unkempt, his wavy chestnut hair rumpled and his thick beard untrimmed. His clothes were that of a traveler or outdoorsman, but his parka and winter boots were of vintage military issue. The man's forehead was beaded with sweat, as if he was coming down from a recent fever.

"The broth's ready," the man said, looking hopefully into the kitchen as the aluminum lid jittered on its pot. Howard stood and poured the steaming broth into a large mug before carefully handing it to his guest. He sat again and asked the man pointedly, "What's your name?"

"Honestly... I don't know," the man said anxiously before taking a long sip of the hot liquid. "I can remember walking down a deserted road and seeing a light in the window of your cabin. I took the path and knocked, but you didn't answer. I started to search for another door when I felt dizzy and fell into the snow. It's really just a blank before then."

"I was getting quite drowsy in that chair," Howard said offhandedly, despite his lingering concern for his guest. "I was starting to nod off... in a kind of waking dream of some old memories... when I heard the noise. The comfort of the fireplace sometimes does that to me. How many times did you knock?"

The man took another sip from his mug after removing his mittens, choosing not to answer Howard's last question. "Am I sick?" he asked instead, lightly touching his forehead with his fingers, a look of bewilderment on his face. "I don't even remember why I was on that road." He sat in silence for a moment before turning to stare at Howard. "Who are you?"

"I'm Howard..." he replied, stopping himself before he gave his full name. *I'm stuck with this fellow until I can get to a phone*, Howard calculated. *He's going to at least spend the night. Whatever he has might be contagious too. Blast!*

"There's nothing you can remember before tonight, young man? Nothing at all?" Howard then queried, hoping for anything that might reveal if his guest was a threat.

The man eagerly finished his cup of broth, reaching down to put the empty mug on the cabin floor. He listlessly surveyed the room before turning back to Howard. "My first memory, which is hazy at best, is of taking a trip to a foreign land," he said in a distant voice, now gazing into the soft, dancing flames of the fireplace. "I'd hired a local guide and we rode on pack camels to a remote region of the country. The guide was about my age, and he wore a head wrapping, a kind of turban, but I can't yet remember his name."

Suddenly intrigued by his guest despite his initial reservations, Howard interjected before the man could continue: "What did the camels look like? I mean, did they have one hump or two humps?" Howard grinned as he said this but was also serious, leaning forward in his chair to better hear the man's reply.

The man furrowed his brow for a moment and then his eyes widened in surprise as the detail came to him. "Two," he said, hesitantly holding up two of his fingers before him. "I remember that now, the camels had two humps." He sat back, seemingly satisfied.

"Then you weren't in Arabia. It was somewhere else. Up in the mountains perhaps?" Howard said, probing the man impatiently. He was beginning to believe the man's story could truly be authentic; he was so obviously reliving a genuine memory hitherto buried in the recesses of his mind.

"Yes," the man replied, cautiously nodding his head. "Yes. We had traveled from the city where I hired my guide and then we rode into the mountains." He spoke more surely now, his confidence growing. "The journey took us several days. We were looking for a site I had found on an old map some years before. I was an explorer, or maybe a professor of antiquities."

"What were you hoping to find there?" Howard interrupted again, feeling himself drawn into the unfolding story and momentarily taken aback by the man's archaic phrasing.

"The answer to a riddle," the man said, the first reply he had given with real conviction. "I'd studied a collection of clay tablets from the same part of the world, found in a long-forgotten cave. Thieves had stolen the tablets at first, but then they were sold at auction. I must have obtained them somehow.

"The tablets told of a lost city in which a great temple was hidden. The city and its temple were ancient even when the tablets were set down. From these tablets, I was able to identify an incomplete map from a special collection, the only map in the world to hint at this city's location.

"A winding riddle was written on the tablets in a dead language, one which, when unraveled, would grant its solver eternal life. The riddle's answer was kept within the hidden temple, set into the very stone of its walls. I doubted this was true, but when I discovered many subtle references in sacred texts to this riddle of immortality, I began to believe that it might be."

Howard was now gripped by his visitor's story, his inquisitiveness again overcoming any sense of fear. "How could solving a riddle make one immortal?" he asked insistently. "Did the tablets explain what was meant by immortality?"

The man gazed at Howard quizzically for a moment. "No, the translation only states that those who decipher the riddle will be 'granted life for all eternity' or, possibly translated another way, 'bound with those whose lives are eternal.'

"We found the city high on a mountain at the edge of a vast desert, erased from any surviving historical record, far from any modern settlement or trade route. My guide claimed the city had been there from a time 'before the word of the Prophet had spread' and that the few local tribesmen stayed away, despite having thoroughly plundered similar places.

"Securing our pack camels, we scaled the worn rocks to the top of the sloping mountain, finding the abandoned city's wind-blasted columns half-buried in the baked earth. My guide refused to enter, babbling in his own tongue, then saying that he would wait for me at the entrance for my return... if I returned.

"I followed the narrow streets past collapsed walls and ruined buildings, empty for perhaps millennia, and finally located the cracked and fragmented steps of the great temple. At either side of the temple's entrance was a winged guardian, chiseled from the hard stone of the immense structure itself. Flashlight in hand and the tablets' translation notes in my satchel, I entered the lightless place to find the key to the riddle.

"I shone my light as I walked the many corridors of the temple, revealing processions of bearded men from an age long past carved into its austere walls. The passages soon led me to a domed chamber with an anvil-shaped altar at its center, a large stone brazier set before it. A row of sculptures lined a wall nearby, each one a figure, but all without faces.

"I opened my satchel, taking my photographs of the cuneiform text on the tablets, and then compared the photos' script to that on the wall behind the figures. The match was exact, but the wall's script seemed to go further. The narrative contained in the tablets was incomplete.

"The concluding line of the riddle preserved on the tablets had been left out. The final part on the wall read, 'Where the fire burns brightest, you will meet your other self." The riddle made more sense with this neglected line included."

Howard felt woozy, his head beginning to pound. He at once steadied himself on the arm of his chair before questioning the man yet again: "What was the full riddle after reading the script on the temple wall? How did the last line change things?"

The man smiled slightly and said, "The riddle wasn't asking for an answer, but leading its reader to a place. That place was the hidden temple in the lost city."

"Tell me the whole riddle," Howard demanded, now almost angry for reasons he couldn't fathom. "What's the full riddle with its final line?"

"The entire riddle is too long to repeat back to you, but I can tell you the closing part, including the line from the wall," the mystery man offered. He then recited the last part of the riddle in a sing-song manner, almost like a nursey rhyme, the glowing light of the fireplace bathing his face as he spoke. Intoning the words, the man's voice took on an eerie, hypnotic quality:

"Time passes, empires rise and fall, but I remain. Men are born and die, peoples rise and fall, but I remain. The mountains erode to dust, the oceans wither to mud, but I remain. I am you, but not you. I live with you, but once you are no more, I remain. Where the fire burns brightest, you will meet your other self."

There was a tense silence. After a moment, the man began speaking in a low voice: "As I examined my photos, something very odd happened. I turned my flashlight to the figures along the wall and one of them seemed to be watching me, the one closest. The sculpture had no face, as I said, only a smooth stone mask, but the spot where its brow should have been had become arched, the space for its mouth curling into a mocking grin.

"I stowed the photographs in my satchel and then beamed the flashlight into the passage from which I had entered the room. I started to walk, quickly at first, but then breaking into a full run as I was chased by a macabre shadow along the passage walls, one that was not my own.

"I fled the temple, traversing the deserted streets of the lost city until I emerged onto the mountain's plateau. My guide was near the cliff facing westward, the dimming sun a backdrop to a rising sandstorm headed toward us.

"'The camels!' he cried to me as I approached. 'We must get them before the storm comes upon us!' Rushing to the side of the mountain, he frantically searched for a path back down to its rubble-strewn base.

"As my guide clambered down from the cliff, I ran to the precipice and looked out over the desert. The approaching sandstorm was almost majestic, its swirling, cyclonic winds tearing up the arid landscape before it with absolute certainty.

"I labored down the rocks to join my guide and our pack animals, nearly slipping as I reached the bottom. He insisted we ride away from the storm, but I told him I doubted it would do much good, with no shelter in the open desert. We rode northward, hoping to circle around, but the storm soon engulfed us anyway."

Howard was on the edge of his chair despite the growing pain in his head, enthralled by events that were somehow strangely familiar to him. "How did you escape the sandstorm?" he asked the man. "I mean, did your guide get out alive?" For a fleeting moment, Howard wondered why he was so engrossed by such a seemingly fantastic tale, one which he now suspected was someone else's altogether.

"No, Abdul—that was his name—and his mount vanished into the eye of the storm as it finally came over us. I fell behind my poor beast of burden, who partially shielded me from the biting sands that cut into us like shards of shattered glass. When the sandstorm eventually passed, my camel was bloody and raw, barely alive.

"I pressed on without them, the early evening becoming night. The next day I wandered in the desert, foolishly hoping my broken compass might steer me back to civilization and safety. I became thirsty, weary, and half-mad from the punishing heat. On the evening of the third day, as I struggled to find a resting place among the burning sands, I came upon a cool oasis in the desert.

"Here I collapsed and crawled to the shimmering pool of water, its surface sheltered from the desert sun by generous palm trees. I drank deeply, choking as my parched mouth and chest seared with a sharp pain. I then lost consciousness, waking again during the nighttime, unsure how many hours or even days had passed.

"I tried to stand, but light-headedness prevented me from doing so. I lay there on the moist sands near the pool, blurred images of the oasis almost all I could see. Only, once—perhaps more than once—I saw a dark figure standing over me, as if waiting for something.

"My next memory is of being lifted onto the back of a camel, one of many in a long caravan. Some traders had found me, telling me I was sick with fever. My luck held, and I returned alive to the city from which Abdul and I had traveled. I was brought to a hospital by my rescuers. I drifted in and out of consciousness for weeks, only becoming coherent again once my fever broke.

"I couldn't tell the doctors my name or where I was from. No passport was found with me as I had lost most of my carried possessions in the sandstorm. I had no memory of my life before I had traveled to that place—

everything had been wiped away by the long fever. The man I had been before was now entirely unknown."

"What an incredible story!" Howard enthused, even as he felt a gnawing discomfort at its uncertain familiarity. "How did you leave that place? Can you remember why you are here now?" As Howard asked this last question, he almost instantly began to regret it.

The man turned to stare at Howard. "You brought me here, Howard," he replied calmly, the cabin suddenly ominously quiet. "Or should I call you Edward? That's the name of your birth, by the way: Edward Hobhouse. You chose Howard as your name once you recovered and began your new life in the town not far from these woods."

Edward stood abruptly, knocking his chair to the floor. "Get out. Get out now, whoever you are," Edward commanded in a quavering voice, gaping at his seated guest in genuine terror.

"Your buried memories have started to return to you, Edward," the man said, undeterred and cold-eyed. "You were beginning to recall your journey to the forbidden city when I knocked on your door. Once your delirium-filled mind became a blank slate at the oasis, I could no longer assume your place and then lost you for many years. You could remember nothing of the riddle of the tablets or the eternal temple after your fever finally broke—that is, not until tonight."

Studying the face of the stranger, Edward realized suddenly who he was. The man was his younger self, bearded and dressed in the clothes of that bygone period, decades before.

Edward bolted toward the cabin door, flinging it open and running out into the howling winds and falling snow. A storm was coming, Edward could see that. The snowfall grew heavy as he ran, frigid winds whipping against his ill-clothed form. Edward glanced over his shoulder and saw the dark silhouette of the stranger striding after him, drawing closer as Edward slowed, now staggering through the deep snow drifts coating the forest floor.

The road to town was close. Edward focused and tried to push himself forward, making one last effort to pull ahead of his pursuer. As he came within reach of his goal, Edward fell, tumbling into a ditch by the roadside.

He lay on his back in the trench, the falling snow stinging his eyes as he struggled weakly to rise. Stepping into the ditch, Edward's doppelgänger stood above him, looking down at the man who had solved the riddle of the tablets and who it would now replace in the world of the living.

The lost city stood empty, obscured by the shifting sands of the desert, but within its temple to the other world, the mirror-world of shadows, there was a momentary disturbance. The brazier at the foot of the altar flared to life and then slowly died, its fire burning brightly for an instant as another soul was taken into the chamber's tabernacle, forever bound by the stone figures watching over it.

The Nest

I t's been months since I've written in this journal. I've been preoccupied with applying to medical schools, and now I've been accepted to the program of my first choice. I've gone on at length about this university and its merits, so I'll restraint myself here.

I've worked so hard for this and now it's happening. Moving across the country will be challenging, as will school, but I feel that I'm prepared for that challenge. When I first decided to practice medicine as a career, I was only a high school student, young and naïve about the sacrifices this decision would require of me. But I now move forward to my future as an adult, a man ready to take his place as part of the medical community.

I wish my parents were alive to see me now. These last few years have been so hard without Mom—not just emotionally, but without her financial support too, I'm sorry to write. School will be costly, but with loans and some academic grants, I'll pull through. I've yet to settle on a specialty, but it'll be a lucrative one, whatever I eventually choose. I was always very handy—Mom said I should be an engineer—but now I'm going to be a doctor instead.

I broke up with Allison this past weekend. She took the news quite hard, I'm also sorry to write. I just felt our relationship wouldn't work long-distance and that she would eventually hold me back from success in the medical profession. Her hope, most likely, was to marry well, and I wish her the best in the years to come, even if I never see her again.

I never really loved her—this was the root cause of our break-up, more than anything else. I would go through the motions, telling her I loved her only when she said the same. But there was no real feeling there, only some attraction, and even that faded after a while. In hindsight, I'm surprised we lasted as long as we did, considering that only one of us was ever really serious about it.

I may meet someone new in medical school, though my first year will certainly be a hectic one. I'm not sure how I feel about marrying another doctor. Are such couples likely to divorce? I'll have to do a quick search and see what I find (the answer is most probably yes). But the university is a large one, and there are many students there from all over the country, if not the world.

August 24th

Today was the first day of class. I have "Gross Anatomy" tomorrow, which will involve dissecting a human cadaver. I'm not entirely sure what to expect from this class, but I've already heard several worrisome (read: disgusting) stories. In any case, I purchased my copy of *Grant's Dissector* from the bookstore today, and I'm ready for it.

One of the other first-year medical students informed me that while some of the cadavers arrive at the medical school as willing donations, many others are "donors by circumstance," meaning that no one claimed the body and that the state ended up giving the remains to the school.

The cadavers are ostensibly screened for infectious diseases beforehand, but I'm not so sure.

That said, I think I've decided to specialize in internal medicine: either oncology or even hematology, which would make me a "blood doctor." Cancer may finally be cured one day, and I'd like to be a part of that—or at least the beneficiary of some cancer research largesse (ha!).

My assigned lab room is across from the school's immunology department, where some of the program's Ph.D. students conduct their dissertation research. I saw a sign outside their office today requesting blood donations and a cohort of subjects for clinical trials. It seems the department is working on an experimental vaccine and needs to evaluate its potential side effects on subjects with certain blood types. I'm interested in the work being done there and would like to meet some of the graduate students. Who knows, something worthwhile may come of it.

August 26th

Anatomy class was yesterday, and I couldn't face eating dinner afterward. Our team's cadaver is in relatively good shape—I'd guess he died in his forties. We won't know the cadaver's documented age or cause of death until the end of the course.

This morning, I stopped by immunology to donate blood with the intention of participating in the experimental vaccine's clinical trials. I'd never given blood before, and I didn't know my blood type (odd, isn't it?).

The study will only select donors from the 'O' and 'A' groups, which constitute most of the general population, and will screen for other variables. There will be another set of clinic trials later for the 'B' group, and potentially the uncommon 'AB' group blood type. The variant of the virus being studied appears to hold a higher chance of infecting some blood types than others, with worse symptoms for those infected from the high-risk blood groups.

The woman administering the blood draw was quite pretty and is a year ahead of me. She said her field will eventually be toxicology. She intends to return to her native country after graduation and work with her father, a physician himself.

I asked her why she was working in immunology, and she revealed her plans to pursue a Ph.D. in the field in addition to an MD. I have to say, I was immediately drawn to her: she's olive-skinned, doe-eyed, and... well, I'll stop there. It's my hope she was flirting with me when she told me her first name, "Aradhya," (spelling?) and then said, "But my friends call me Andi," smiling coyly. I'll know the results of the tests next week.

September 2nd

My blood type is "Vel-negative," one of the rarest known blood types! I always knew I was special, but this is a surprise. Andi seemed pleased as well and said the department might contact me some time for a study of seronegative subjects in unusual blood groupings.

I wanted to ask Andi out on a date before I left, but she was pulled away by the department's PI after giving me my results. Maybe I'll see her around on campus. Hopefully soon.

September 13th

I was walking back from class this afternoon when I saw Andi. She approached an empty bench with some textbooks, a large flock of pigeons abruptly scattering as she took her seat. This was quite strange—the few others seated on benches nearby hadn't perturbed the feeding birds.

She didn't seem to notice me. I walked up to her bench and then announced, "I would use an old pick-up line, but you already know my blood type."

Andi looked up, smiled, and then laughed. Corny, I know, but it worked. We're having dinner this weekend.

September 17th

We ate at a restaurant of her choosing, a hole-in-the-wall place with candles in wine bottles on the tables. Andi said it was "cozy," but I thought it was just dark. The waiter seated us in the back, where it was quiet, which was fine with me.

After finishing our meal, we talked about medical school, her home overseas, her family, and her research interests. She did most of the talking, as I'm not fully comfortable discussing my past. Her family seems quite well-off, if not wealthy, and I don't want her to possibly dismiss me as unsuitable before we've grown closer. She's beautiful, and I could become quite serious about her.

As the sun began to set outside, shadows drew over our table, Andi's face now only partially visible in the flickering candlelight. Her voice grew distant, and I felt myself nodding off, the lids of my eyes becoming heavy. There seemed to be a second voice whispering to me, even as Andi spoke at length, hissing in some secret, unknown language...

It could've only been my overtaxed mind. I sat up and apologized to Andi, saying that I must have almost dozed for a moment. The stress of medical school, even early in the semester. She said she didn't notice anything and thanked me for listening to her for so long, that she didn't have many friends even after more than a year at school. Andi said she would like to see me again, maybe even during the week if she had time. I was thrilled—I felt pulled to her, and I didn't even consider refusing.

December 10th

My final exams are done. My grades have been slipping as I've been spending more time with Andi, but I still feel confident I'll finish in the top quarter of my class this semester. Onto the next set of courses.

Andi and I have been meeting each other as time allows, she being more studious than even myself. We've gone on several more dates around town, and I hope to see her again once we return from winter break. She said she'll be flying home for the next few weeks to visit her parents.

I think about her often when we're not together, which is distracting. I wouldn't say it's an obsession; more of an infatuation. She's shown up in some of the dreams I can hazily recall after waking, and I find myself daydreaming about her even in class (bad). Things will ramp up next semester, but I want to keep seeing her. I can think of almost nothing else.

January 7th

I met Andi yesterday after class and she said she wanted a break for a few months. That we both needed to focus more on school. I reluctantly agreed and said we could at least meet for lunch occasionally, on campus. She said she would call me once she found her footing under her current course load, maybe at the beginning of next month.

That night, I dreamt about Andi again, but I can remember the entire dream this time, in detail. We were somewhere in a jungle (weird), at the entrance to an overgrown and dilapidated palace. Andi stood at the entrance and bid me follow her, but I stayed put. She then began a seductive dance in response, her arms sensually writhing and undulating as she gazed at me. The strange, shrill whispering I had heard on our first date filled my ears, and I felt I had to obey...

My overactive imagination! Andi's right: we need to concentrate on medical school and make it through this semester. But I hope to spend some time with her again soon.

April 9th

I spent the night at Andi's apartment last night. We had met earlier that evening for our first real date since last semester. Over dinner, Andi looked lovely and glowing; she had never been more desirable to me.

She also seemed happy and rested, as if she was more assured of her academic progress. We'd met several times over the past few months for campus lunch dates, where we mostly talked about our classes. The last time, Andi had suggested a date night soon, "as the weather is getting warmer."

After our dinner date, I walked her home and she invited me up. She is an amazing, intoxicating woman, unlike anyone I've ever met. I believe, for the first time in my life, that I might be in love. I'd do anything for her and be glad to do it.

June 7th

As soon as my last exam was written, I received a call from Andi. She told me she had to meet with me, her voice strangely nervous. I asked her why the urgency, and she said she had to tell me in person.

So, I find out that Andi's pregnant. She's known since last month but didn't want to tell me as exams were coming up. I asked her what she wanted to do, and she said, "Get married." I'd not wanted it to happen this way, but I'd already been considering proposing to her, just not so soon. And now I'm going to be a father, even as I have three more years of medical school to complete.

June 8th

Andi called me again today, this time telling me that we have to travel outside the country over the summer break. The plane will leave this Saturday, apparently, the day after both of us get our final grades. Andi assured me we would be back in plenty of time for the fall semester, but that we had to meet her parents. "Otherwise, they just won't understand," she told me before hanging up the phone.

June 10th

I'm writing this from the airport. I did well on my exams, but not as well as I had hoped. I've brought next semester's textbooks with me just in case; I can't stop studying even for a few weeks. Andi didn't tell me about her exams or how she did. She must be too worried about her pregnancy.

We took a taxi here and I noticed as she got in that Andi was already wearing maternity clothes, even though it's only been a few months. She is quite visibly pregnant; maybe it's bloating, but it seems peculiar. We haven't slept together since last month (exams and all), so I can't really tell how much her body has changed.

June 12th

We landed in the early afternoon local time and then took a car to our hotel. Andi had apparently made the arrangements before we left. This city is a huge slum, I must say. While there are some signs of modernity, the trash, the beggars, the air and noise pollution, etc., are overwhelming. I couldn't wait to arrive here as our hotel, at least, is clean and well-appointed. Andi says we'll leave for her family's home in the countryside late tomorrow morning, after we've had some breakfast.

June 15th or June 16th?

I don't know how many days have passed, to be honest, so the recorded dates are only a guess. I was able to recover my journal, as it had been left in our rented car along with some of our luggage. I couldn't carry the suitcases – even so, it wasn't really an option - and instead grabbed a knapsack with my journal inside as I made my escape.

I question my sanity after the events of the last several days. I need to write this all down, as I'm not sure what I believe that I witnessed really happened. We left for Andi's family's home before noon on the 13th and drove for several hours. The driving was hard going as it's monsoon season and the waterlogged dirt roads are treacherous.

When I wrote earlier that I suspected Andi's family was wealthy, I wasn't wrong. Her family's "home" is more of a palace, but one shrouded by the surrounding jungle. The isolation is due to her family's lineage, Andi explained when we arrived. It was only later that I found out exactly what that meant.

We were greeted by servants at the gates, who then parked our car in the circular driveway. Her parents were genial and seemed genuinely happy to see me. We ate an early dinner in the dining room and then settled into a room that could probably be considered the parlor to discuss wedding plans.

Her father, who when not speaking seemed very stern, eventually said that the wedding must take place there, in the family home, and that relatives and friends would attend. I asked him when the wedding would take place, and he said "tonight."

Needless to say, I was taken aback. Andi had never mentioned any plans for a wedding so soon. I also didn't see any other guests anywhere in the house. When I asked about them, Andi only said the wedding guests were "downstairs."

After our conversation, Andi and her father withdrew from the parlor and seemed to disappear. I spoke with Andi's mother for a while, who mostly asked me about medical school and some other personal matters, and then she left as well, saying the servants would fetch me soon.

I roamed the halls near the parlor, noting the unusual décor. The paintings on the walls were not what I had expected; one appeared very old, and showed a snake charmer playing his flute, a cobra rising from its basket at his command. Nothing in the home's art revealed the family's religion, and Andi had never said what faith she practiced, if any.

A servant appeared, an old man, who said he would lead me to the reception. I passed a window as we left the hallway; night had fallen. The man opened a heavy door leading to stairs and I followed them down to a narrow hall that wound beneath the house, ending in yet another door and then another hallway. At the end of the second hall was a burning torch in a wall fixture, dimly illuminating a third and final door. The man took the torch from its holder and opened the door, gesturing for me to enter this dark place.

I walked out onto the plateau of a cavern, one which spread out before me. The servant stood behind me with his torch, making sure I didn't try to leave as he closed the door. Below us were dozens of people, the "wedding guests," all holding lit torches of their own. We made our way down a flight of stone steps to the bottom of the high-vaulted cavern, a dais made of the same harsh stone rising at its center.

Andi's father appeared from among the crowd, his eyes and cheeks daubed with white paint in some ceremonial fashion. There were two circles around his eyes joined together by a curved line that ended at his chin. I then noticed that every member of the gathered throng displayed these same face-painted spectacles.

He held out his hand to me, saying, "Here is the groom. Come to me, my son, take your seat and meet your bride, my daughter." Above me, on the stone dais, was a high-backed chair, a kind of throne. Andi's father led me to the chair and I sat down, not knowing whether they were mad or whether this really was some strange foreign custom.

Andi's father then said I belonged to an ancient bloodline, one apparently associated with many places I had never even heard of (where is Lemuria?). He daubed my face with the same white paint he and the guests wore, making the same two circular marks and connecting line. As he finished his work, I heard the sound of something large moving from the shadows beyond the light of the torches, something slithering on its belly.

An enormous brown snake appeared before the dais, rearing its head and flicking its forked tongue as I gazed up at it. The hooded snake was easily thirty feet long and heavy-bodied, long enough to wrap itself entirely around the dais where I sat.

I don't quite remember what happened next. I perhaps screamed or tried to flee—there's a black spot in my memory. My mind... Where was Andi? I was then held by two men, one on each arm, restraining me as the snake coiled itself at the foot of the throne. It watched me, its reptilian eyes devoid of any feeling, yet somehow intent.

The female snake began to lay its brood of eggs, one after the other, into the soil gathered in a loose pile on the dais. Nearby, at the dais's edge, was a copper vessel of some kind, something which could hold the newly laid eggs if needed.

Once the pregnant snake had laid its clutch, it hovered over me and fanned its hood as if beckoning the others.

The mob stepped onto the dais, shouting with joy, dancing wildly as if in celebration. They then began to chant—a strange song in a language I didn't recognize, hypnotic, the monstrous snake swaying to its rhythm as the guests repeated its words again and again.

I was led away by the two men who had restrained me to a wood cage fitted with iron bars. They pushed me inside, one of the men locking its barred door. The crowd filed up the stone steps out of the cavern, a line of torches lighting their exit. My prison was not far from the dais, and I could see the snake coiled around its eggs.

The men who'd imprisoned me hadn't searched me thoroughly. I had my multi-tool pocket-knife, something I always keep with me. The snake looked asleep around its eggs, or at least supine.

I reached through the bars of the cage and worked its old lock with my pocket tool's short blade. The lock clicked, and I cautiously eased open the door. Several torches in holders still threw light about the cavern, and I reached for one of them as I approached the sleeping snake.

I struck the snake with my fiery torch. It recoiled in shock, slithering away from its eggs and then falling off the dais. I leaped down after it, swinging with the torch, the snake trying to strike but being beaten down by the fire as I struck again and again. I took my knife and stabbed into its eye, pulling the blade free and stabbing again, cutting its head and throat until, finally, it was dead. The snake made no sound as it lay on the cavern floor, dark blood oozing from its wounds in the faint torchlight.

The brood of eggs. I scooped up the soil around them with my hands, dumping it into the copper vessel until it was mostly full. I carefully put the multitude of eggs into the container, making sure each of the soft, white ovals was unbroken and secure. Were these my children? Was the snake that I had just killed... was that Andi? My mind...

The door from the cavern was unlocked. I made my way down the halls, vessel in hand, leaving the nighttime house as both its owners and their servants slept or celebrated or plotted, I know not which. Andi had driven us here, so I had no keys to our car. But its doors were open, so I grabbed my knapsack and fled into the jungle.

I'm not sure where I am now. They may be looking for me. I managed to find a palm hut after only a few hours of stumbling through the underbrush, and it's here where I write in this journal. I need to keep the eggs warm. When they hatch, I'll be able to be with them—my children—in their nest. So many of them.

It's raining outside, so hard I can scarcely hear myself think. How long will it take? I don't know. Sometimes I think I hear Andi's voice, calling to me from the darkness outside. Isn't she dead? All I can do now is wait and hope they don't find me. Not before my children hatch.

Things that Go Bump in the Night

T he night was very still, but then Thomas woke. He yawned, surprised he had woken at such a late hour after his early bedtime. He rose from his bed and pushed open his sparsely furnished bedroom's window, the moon fuller than he'd seen it for a long time. There was nothing close to his family's house save the bramble woods behind it, which had so far remained unexplored. There was time —after all, they'd only moved in a few weeks ago.

Thomas and his parents had traveled across the country to their new home near his mother's hometown. Mother had taken ill lately, and the doctor had advised a warmer climate to aid in her recovery, so the family uprooted themselves. Thomas's father planned to set up shop in the nearby town while his mother recuperated. They might stay forever, even if Mother did become well again, as there was no local blacksmith.

The house sat along a country road, miles from town and the homes of the neighbors. Occasionally a horse and buggy would ride by and, every once in a while, one of those fancy Model Ts would sputter past, leaving a noxious trail behind it. The place was old—no one had lived there for years, though it had been maintained by an estate agency somewhere out east.

Near to the house was an overgrown abandoned cemetery sheltered by the perimeter of the woods. Thomas had caught glimpses of the cemetery's rusted ornamental gates as he passed, but he had never really given the place much thought. Tonight, however, the moon was so bright Thomas could see many of the cemetery's headstones, as well as the moss-covered mausoleums at the back of the plot.

Distracted by the tranquil evening, Thomas didn't notice the thing moving in the cemetery until it came directly into his view. He leaned forward for a better look, his head emerging from the window.

A very tall and gaunt man, dressed entirely in black funeral garb, strode purposefully through the cemetery grounds. He was followed by two other men, one short and squat and the other broad and hunched. The moon's pure light flooded the cemetery, casting long shadows behind the three men as they weaved between the gravestones.

The ghastly trio stopped at a headstone and then began to dig, the sounds muffled but still audible from Thomas's perch. The tall man stood over the other two as they labored, their shovels scraping against the rocky soil with each thrust. As they dug, the tall man suddenly tilted his head from the open grave and looked straight at Thomas, his eyes seemingly fixed on him.

Thomas froze, unsure whether the specter-like man was gazing at him or merely looking up at the house. The tall man then slowly smiled, giving him a wide, sinister grin, erasing any doubt Thomas felt. The hairs on the back of Thomas's neck stood on end, a chill unlike any he had felt before crawling up his spine.

The tall man then abruptly turned away, gesturing toward his henchmen. A coffin had been exhumed by their work, encrusted with dirt and bound in heavy chains. The two diggers lifted the disinterred coffin by its handles and the tall man followed them among the trees, the thick oaks of the deeper woods obscuring their destination.

Thomas had been holding his breath, but now exhaled. He scanned the woods again for any sign of movement and then sat down on his bed, the mattress springs squeaking under his weight.

Those men, they looked almost like corpses! Thomas thought, now taking measured breaths as he opened the top buttons of his long nightshirt. Hoping no one was in the cemetery to see, he turned the knob of the gas lamp resting on his dresser, the dark room lighting with a soft hiss.

The lamp basked the bedroom in a warm glow. Thomas stretched his legs over the edge of his mattress and waited for his nerves to regain some semblance of calm. He stood to shut the bedroom window, peeking to see if the men had returned, his shadow large against the unadorned walls of the room.

After some time, Thomas turned out the light, the silence of the house assuring him his parents hadn't woken. He thought of the wan, cadaverous features of the nighttime visitors as he drifted back into sleep. They'd been closer to animals than human beings.

"Here, Mr. Hughes, just sign on this line and then here as well," the estate agent said, coolly professional but, as Thomas sensed, in something of a hurry. Thomas had received the man's telegram soon after returning home from the war, which was now thankfully over. Thomas had seen some action on the Western Front, but only after the fighting had moved out of the trenches.

The telegram informed Thomas that his father had died while overseas. Mother had died years earlier, shortly after moving into the house. She was taken by a wasting illness, one which hadn't been ameliorated by the mild climate of the coast. Thomas's father had been so broken by the loss that he fell into a deep depression from which he never truly recovered. He'd sent Thomas away to live with his aunt and uncle, who'd raised him to adulthood.

"And here are the keys to the house, Mr. Hughes," the estate agent, a Mr. Betts, said, offering a small keyring to Thomas. Thomas placed the keyring in his suit vest pocket for easy access. "I'm also sorry about your father, Mr. Hughes," Mr. Betts said, his tone softening somewhat. "The agency tells me he was buried in the church cemetery in town, and no one attended the funeral. You should visit his grave to pay your respects before taking your leave of this place."

"My father wasn't close to the family, Mr. Betts," Thomas replied, reluctant to share anything personal with a stranger but believing it necessary in this case. "After my mother passed away, my father was seized by a melancholy disposition—it seemed to eat away at him. We rarely spoke after I was taken in by his sister and her husband—and, of course, I've been away these last few years."

"A few of the locals tell me the elder Hughes was fearful of something, living out here in isolation," Mr. Betts said quietly, his formerly reserved manner now hinting at a kind of nervousness. "Cars would drive past at night and there were strange lights in the windows, even at the oddest of times."

"Just some country gossip, Mr. Betts," Thomas replied, seeking to reassure the estate agent. "If my father was in danger or something like that, he would have just moved away. He kept up his blacksmith shop until fairly recently, as I understand it."

Once the estate agent had said his goodbyes, Thomas watched him drive off down the bumpy dirt road not far from his newly acquired house. Selling the property to an interested party would take some doing as the location was not a favorable one. Thomas had had to take the bus and then hitch a ride with a farmer to get there in the first place, but now he could drive his father's old Model T. The car was garaged nearby, in a small barn within view of that creepy abandoned cemetery.

The memory of that strange night years ago had haunted Thomas ever since, but he rarely consciously thought of it. After going to live with his aunt and uncle, Thomas had sometimes had nightmares of the scene in the cemetery, the bestial faces of those men hovering over him as he slept. With maturity, the nightmares faded, and Thomas hadn't dwelt on that night since. That is, not until his first night sleeping in the old house.

Fluffing his pillow, Thomas lay on the same bed he had slept in as a boy. He'd found his boyhood room almost bare except for a bed frame and mattress with its dresser and lamp. Still, he'd been able to find some bedsheets and pillows in the hall closet. Now, laid down for the night, he wondered momentarily if that scene from his childhood might repeat itself.

Thomas woke suddenly, shafts of luminous moonlight pouring in through the bedroom window. Still tired from the previous day of travel, Thomas was surprised by how awake he felt. He sat up under his bedsheets. Pulling himself from the creaking bedframe, he walked to the open window, resting against the sill to view the woods behind the house.

The three men were at work in the cemetery. They had just pulled a chain-bound coffin from its upturned grave and were now placing it on solid earth. As Thomas watched the scene unfold, the tall man, the dwarf, and the hunchback all paused their efforts and turned to look up toward the house. They stared right at Thomas and smiled, their soulless grins so terrifying as to be the stuff of nightmares themselves.

Thomas fell back across the small room and slammed into a wall, dropping to the floor in a heap. His palms were plastered against his temples as he noiselessly screamed, the disquieting horror of that night years ago returning to him in an instant. The shadowy bedroom began to spin around him in dizzying circles and then was swallowed by blackness.

Thomas woke on the bedroom floor, the rays of the morning sun shining on his face. He lay crumpled in a corner of the room, a shallow gash across his forehead from where he had fallen the night before. After staggering to his feet, Thomas put on his pants and shoes and walked outside to the small well in the front yard. He placed his head under the pump's spout, dousing it with cold gushing water until he felt fully alert and right in his mind again.

He toweled off in front of a hall mirror and examined the gash, wondering if it might need stitches. *I'm going into those woods today while it's light. I'll find where the monster men are taking the coffins*, Thomas thought to himself, feeling the dull pain of his wound but still ready to confront his childhood terror. Thomas had never been sure if what he'd seen that night was real, but now he knew.

Fully dressed except for his suit coat, Thomas put his Colt service revolver in its leather holster under his arm and went to the cemetery, stopping at its battered gates. *Why do they bury the dead so far away from town?* Thomas considered. *This place seems like it hasn't been used in decades. I wonder why it's here?*

The rusted gates opened part way with some effort and Thomas slipped into the cemetery. The plot hadn't been cared for in many years, its sinking headstones being nearly engulfed by purplish vines, putrid-hued mosses, and sickly lichens. The names on the stones were mostly obscured by both age and the overgrowth, but all the ones

Thomas inspected seemed to bear the same family name: de San Martín.

The name sounded Catholic to Thomas, but there was no evidence of Christian imagery on the headstones or anywhere else in the cemetery. In fact, Thomas couldn't find any religious iconography at all. Two of the mausoleums at the back of the plot carried this family name engraved above their ponderous doors. The largest of the three structures, however, bore only one man's name, that of Ignacio de San Martín.

As he left the cemetery to explore the woods beyond, Thomas searched for the disturbed grave he'd seen last night. None could be found—the soil around the gravestones appeared untouched by anyone, still covered in the weed-like grass that grew throughout the cemetery plot.

There was no clear path through the woods, so Thomas looked for spots of low foliage over which to tread. As he progressed, the woods became denser, the hanging, invasive vines now almost black and the heavy oaks gradually contorting into agonized poses. Thorny underbrush tore at Thomas's clothes, his shirt and pant legs repeatedly caught by barbs. At last, he spotted through the leaves of the trees what appeared to be a sprawling house.

The faint outline of an alabaster stone footpath led from the colonial-style mansion and disappeared past Thomas deeper into the woods. The house itself, once resplendent in adobe-white and red, was now quite dilapidated. It looked like it had been abandoned long ago, just like the cemetery.

The front doors, to Thomas's surprise, were unlocked and he stepped into the foyer of the hacienda. The sun lit the murky place through sporadic holes in its raised ceiling, bathing the ruin in dim orange light. The floor of the estate was mostly covered with debris from the building itself and its furniture, and a wrought-iron staircase led up to the second level.

Thomas heard a high-pitched tittering sound as he stepped into the first floor's center. Listening closely, he discovered that the noise was coming from the nearby wall, or so it seemed. The tittering then grew louder—the sound seemed to be coming from everywhere, even from above.

Are they rats? Thomas worried as he looked down, hoping none were at his feet. Thomas also considered they might be nesting birds—only, he'd seen no signs of animal life as he drew near to the mansion.

Ascending the unsteady staircase, his hand on its rail, Thomas walked along the open second floor. He paused at a portrait that had fallen from its place along the wall and now rested upright. The walls here were lined with many pictures of the family who had occupied the house, but this one stood out to Thomas.

The daguerreotype was that of a young woman, taken sometime during the last century. Despite the portrait's age, the woman in the picture held a notable resemblance to his late mother. Almost everything about them was the same, save for the clothes of the period.

Thomas had never met his maternal grandparents, nor had he ever seen a youthful picture of his mother. He knew her family was from this area (it was why they had moved here in the first place), but his mother had died before she could introduce Thomas and his father to "the family."

There was an iron-bound wooden door leading to an adjoined tower, which Thomas had thought only a folly from the outside. The tittering from earlier had subsided, but now became quite noticeable as Thomas opened the tower door, as if the rats in the walls were becoming agitated. He climbed the worn steps until he came to a circular room at the tower's top.

It was an embalming chamber of some sort, with workbenches and iron-manacled tables for subjects. Scattered over a table in no certain order were books and scrolls, some in languages Thomas didn't recognize.

Dirt from possibly the grave thinly coated one of the manacled tables. *Fresh?* Thomas wondered. *Is this an undertaker's lab? An alchemist's study?* He felt as excited at his discovery as he was perplexed by it.

Thomas picked up one of the few titled books from the table and began to turn through its foul-smelling pages. The book was a treatise on vivisection and bloodletting, written in the antiquated English of several centuries ago. One page displayed a diagram of a man's body, the body parts labeled in an incomprehensible script.

Leafing ahead, Thomas paused at one line in particular: *The flesh and vital organs of the young man of shared blood are to be fed to those afflicted, so as to revive them to sound body and good health.*

A loud crashing sound shattered the silence. It had come from downstairs. Thomas put the moldy book under his arm and hurried down the tower steps, unbuttoning his holster for quick access to his service revolver. The rats in the walls were now tittering in a frenzy, scurrying about and scratching as Thomas descended the staircase and then ran out through the decaying mansion's doors.

More time had passed than Thomas had initially supposed. The early fall sun was beginning to set over his house. He squinted in the low light, exhausted from his return trip through the dense woods surrounding the derelict mansion.

He ate several sandwiches he had left in the icebox at the kitchen table, the gas lamp suspended above his head flickering occasionally. Satisfied, he went upstairs and lay across his bed in the dark, the strange book he had taken from the tower resting on the dresser nearby.

Mother is somehow intertwined in all of this, I just know it, Thomas thought to himself, the doubts he had always had about her becoming firmer after the day's disturbing excursion. *Mother has to be the woman in that picture! There's no other explanation.*

Thomas's memories of his mother were vague, but something he did remember with certainty was her often cold manner, punctuated by perhaps feigned episodes of warmth. Mother had sometimes seemed as if she was assessing him and his father for some unknown purpose. This behavior grew more obvious as time passed, especially in the months before the family relocated.

Thomas rose from the bed and entered his parents' room, turning on the gas lamp that perched atop a dresser. He searched the bedroom dressers and found nothing, all of his father's clothes and belongings having been taken after his sudden death.

Opening the large walk-in closet, he found nothing but wire hangers left along its wooden rod. Thomas then sat on the barren mattress and stared into the empty closet space, wondering where else he might search.

In the dim light, Thomas noticed the faint outline of an irregular panel along the back of the closet. He stood and parted the hangers, reaching out to knock on the panel. *Hollow.*

Bending a wire hanger into a tool, he pried the panel loose, revealing a crevice containing a leather-bound notebook. It was a diary—his mother's. Thomas grabbed the book from its hiding place and began to quickly turn through its pages:

The deception has worked. James and my son, Thomas, have followed me to the family grounds unaware. I am truly ill, and I'm not sure how much time I have left, but Thomas's sacrifice will make the family well again, including myself.

Only some of us can move about as normal, in the daylight. So many of the family have been reduced to little more than beasts, stunted animals that inhabit the burrows and warrens beneath the estate. But for myself, that I could bear a child at my advanced age is astounding, a revelation that inspired Uncle Gaspar to hatch this desperate plan. I may be the last de San Martín female to have produced issue until our family's degeneration is reversed.

Once we are ready, those who are buried in the family plot, as well as the rest of the de San Martín clan, will be made whole, undoing the effects of centuries of consanguineous unions and the corrupting powers of the dark arts. Even our patriarch, Ignacio de San Martín, will be roused from his torpor, hearing and dreaming but dormant while interred in his crypt, to rejoin the family he first led into our Master's service.

The stairs leading to the first floor of the house creaked from behind the closed door of the bedroom. Thomas put aside the diary and slowly drew his firearm from its holster, counting six rounds in its chambers.

Thomas threw open the bedroom door and fired into the hallway. The deformed shape of a man groaned and fell to the floor, lying face down after taking two shots to the chest. Stepping over the body of the hunchback, Thomas crept down the stairs to search for the other two grave robbers who had finally come for him.

In the house's lightless kitchen, Thomas turned slowly, waiting for an attack from the shadows. The dwarf leaped at him, having been concealed in the dark corners of the room. The half-human creature snarled as it dove forward, grasping at Thomas as it took hold of him.

Unable to fire in time, Thomas punched at the dwarf as it bit down hard on his free arm, sinking its jagged teeth into the flesh under his shirt. Thomas cried out, his wound burning as he shook the dwarf free.

The dwarf fell onto the kitchen floor, knocking over a chair as it collided with the table. Thomas aimed in the dark, aided only by the kitchen's moonlit window, and shot the cowering dwarf twice. The first bullet passed through the dwarf's cheek and the second penetrated its eye, the abomination's gnarled hands falling slack as it died.

Thomas ran out through the front door of the house and into the yard. An open coffin, its lid against its side, lay near the porch steps as if waiting for him. Thomas spun and scanned the grounds, his revolver braced and ready.

The tall man was nowhere to be seen. Keeping his revolver in front of him, Thomas circled the perimeter of the house, his eyes searching the high bushes and other hiding places around its foundation. There was no hint of anyone nearby, only the nighttime sounds of the woods piercing the silence.

He has to be here, Thomas thought to himself. *Those other two took his orders. They're all members of the same inbred family—my own family!*

He thought back to the stories his father had told him about his mother. That they had met when his father had left home to travel to a new town to begin his apprenticeship. That his mother had been the one to introduce herself to his father. And that his mother's family lived far away, too far for them to ever really visit.

The sound of falling shingles startled Thomas as the tall man leaped from the roof, striking him on the back with both of his boot heels. Thomas fell forward and dropped his revolver, stunned by the sudden blow to his shoulder blades.

The tall man struck Thomas with a closed fist as he rolled over to face his attacker. The hard punch made Thomas see stars, and he spat blood onto his white shirt as the tall man grabbed him by the throat.

He doesn't want to kill me. The thought flashed through Thomas's mind as he felt his breath being squeezed out of his body by the tall man's unyielding grasp. *They still need me for their ritual.*

Thomas was lifted upward, his feet dangling in the air as his vision grew blurry. He kicked forward and felt his foot connect with a face before dropping to the ground. Dazed, Thomas stood up and saw the tall man sprawled back, the swift kick having taken him by surprise.

He went for his revolver, grasping it from the dirt and managing to fire one rushed shot. The bullet whizzed past the tall man as he leaped again at Thomas, his black cape unfurled. Knocked down by the tall man's punishing fists, Thomas fired into his adversary's chest, a trail of smoke wafting from the barrel as he spent his last bullet. The tall man paused his assault, staggered by the gaping wound, then took an unsteady step backward.

His ammunition gone, Thomas charged and smashed the butt of his revolver into the tall man's sharp nose, knocking off his great uncle's silken top hat. Thomas struck again and again in a frenzy, breaking the ghoulish face of Gaspar de San Martín, a malignant tumor who should have perished centuries ago.

When the figure finally stilled, Thomas rose, panting. Bruised and bloodied, he went to the small barn that garaged his father's Model T. From the toolbox in the trunk, he took a crowbar and a dull knife. There were also two full jugs of kerosene. With some difficulty, Thomas took these as well.

Stalking through the woods past the cemetery at night was an ordeal, but Thomas let the moon and his own memory guide him. The barbs and thorns of the almost-impenetrable thickets tore at him as he neared the mansion grounds, only the clanking of the kerosene bottles breaking the same hushed silence he had encountered on his first trip.

The stark mansion stood before Thomas, its alabaster stone path illuminated by moonlight. He went to its now-closed doors and broke in with the crowbar, battering the lock until it gave way. Entering, he strode to the center of the grand drawing-room, the once sumptuous furniture that littered its floors now only kindling for the fire Thomas planned to set.

Thomas splashed the first jug of kerosene about, the tittering in the walls and the ceiling above reaching a fever pitch as the regressed members of the de San Martín ancestral line realized what was about to happen. As Thomas emptied the second kerosene jug onto the mound of debris, the tittering around him became almost deafening, drowning out Thomas's own manic thoughts.

A lit match was flung onto the pile, instantly igniting into a bonfire and quickly spreading, beginning to consume the rotting walls of the mansion. Thomas fled the house of his antecedents, a place that had seen so much wickedness and suffering; a place that was now the funeral pyre of his family, both living and undead.

He stood at the edge of the woodlands in front of the mansion, watching the structure burn steadily to the ground in a cleansing fire. The evil that had nested there was now being purified, the shrill, piping shrieks of his horrid family ringing into the still night of the dark woods. Thomas de San Martín laughed maniacally as the mansion disappeared behind a wall of flame: a strange, unrestrained laughter that would not stop until the morning light came.

About the Author

James Dermond is a writer who lives in Colorado. Intrigued from a very young age by horror anthologies and the short story form, he offers this book as his latest modest contribution to the genre.

Doorways to the Unseen 3: 6 Tales of Terror and Suspense is the third volume in a series of short story collections. The fourth volume in the series will be published in early 2022.

To sign up for free eBooks and other future giveaways, please subscribe to James Dermond's author website here: www.jamesdermond.com

James Dermond's Amazon Page
https://www.amazon.com/James-Dermond/e/B01M1S54YP

James Dermond's Goodreads Page
https://www.goodreads.com/author/show/15862747.James_Dermond

James Dermond on Facebook
https://www.facebook.com/JamesDermondAuthor/

James Dermond on Twitter
https://twitter.com/JamesDermond

Postscript

Thank you for reading this latest volume in the short horror story series, Doorways to the Unseen! We are now on volume three of what will eventually become a twelve-volume series of books. The planned publication schedule is two volumes every year for the next four years, with the final volume released in early 2026. A multi-volume hardcover edition of the collected stories would then be released later in the same year.

If you enjoyed this collection of stories, please leave a review on Amazon and other online bookstores where volumes in the Doorways to the Unseen series can be found. A positive review will help promote the book and inform other readers of the book's merits.

www.ingramcontent.com/pod-product-compliance
Lightning Source LLC
Chambersburg PA
CBHW020423130626
46549CB00006B/2702